Praise for Alexis Fleming's *Project: MAN*

4 Nymphs "...entertaining and tension filled. The characters are fun and sexy and it's the surprises they have in store that keeps the reader glued to the pages. Ms. Fleming has a gift for details, making her stories easy to visualize. The vivid characterization in this lustful and loving read keeps the smooth progress flowing to the emotion filled end." ~ *Water Nymph, Literary Nymphs Reviews*

"For an enticing tale of love filled with Egyptian artifacts, danger and betrayal don't miss PROJECT: MAN. I highly recommend it." ~ *Lori Ann, RRT Erotic*

4 Stars! "For a story that was so humorous, it was also surprisingly sensuous: teasing, tension building and finally satisfying. If you enjoy old screwball type comedy with an element of suspense, then you will enjoy *Project: MAN*." ~ *Kirra Pierce, Just Erotic Romance Reviews*

4 Lips! "PROJECT: MAN had me laughing out right from the very beginning! The chemistry between Emily and Nicholas is undeniable and the farce that he's forced to act out kept me thoroughly entertained. This fun full-length novel by Alexis Fleming reads quickly." ~ Kerin, Two Lips Reviews

"Project: Man is a very entertaining novel full of engaging characters and an intriguing plot line. The characters were so well drawn that I found myself smiling at their happy times, and feeling their pain at the problems. Ms. Fleming has written a novel that will wrap itself around a reader's heart and seep inside to become a part of them. *Project: Man* is an excellent read, and has earned a place on my keeper shelf" ~ *Amelia, Joyfully Reviewed*

4 Angels *"Project: Man* had me laughing from the first page. Emily is an educated, lovable woman who manages to mistake or misstep with humorous results. Her quirks lend personality to her character and ensure that Nicholas will never be bored. Nicholas is a wonderful compliment to Emily. I thoroughly enjoyed seeing him taken from his element and at a loss on how to interact with Emily. The camaraderie between them is fun, but when paired with the intense sexual tension between them, they become a great couple. The plot is well balanced with plenty of romance, humor, and suspense. The villain may not surprise some readers, but for the most part they won't mind. Ms. Fleming's tale will touch your hearts and leave you smiling." ~ *Amanda, Fallen Angel Reviews*

4 Cups "This is a very funny story. There are quite a few laugh-out-loud moments in this story and I really enjoyed it." ~ *Maura, Coffee Time Romance*

Project: MAN

Alexis Fleming

A Samhain Publishing, Ltd. publication.

Samhain Publishing, Ltd.
512 Forest Lake Drive
Warner Robins, GA 31093
www.samhainpublishing.com

Project: MAN

Print ISBN: 1-59998-364-8
Digital ISBN: 1-59998-171-8

Editing by Angie James
Cover by Scott Carpenter

First Samhain Publishing, Ltd. electronic publication: November 2006
First Samhain Publishing, Ltd. print publication: February 2007

Dedication

To Sunny. My best friend. My soul sister. My life is richer with you in it.

Chapter One

"You're shitting me, right? What on earth do you expect me to do with a man?" Emily planted her hands on her hips and stared across the desk.

The two men perched on the edge of their chairs started to fidget and averted their eyes. Federal Agent Tomlins' slightly plump face and chubby body made him look like an overdressed cherub. The cherub sniggered.

His partner, Federal Agent Banks, was a much younger man, with baby-face looks and the cocky arrogance of someone very conscious of his position. It was pathetically clear to Emily he was trying to emulate his older colleague. Without the life experience and added years, he came off as brash and officious.

"Okay, I have been kind of...spooked since I found the papyrus in the Egyptian pot I got for my birthday." She directed her words toward the more senior of the agents. "But I thought it was my imagination."

"Explain spooked," Agent Tomlins snapped.

Emily frowned. "It's difficult, but I just feel something isn't right. I've tried to pin it down, but I can't get a handle on it."

"Has someone approached you about the papyrus?"

"No, but I've had a feeling someone has been watching me. Both here *and* at my house. And I kind of sensed that someone had followed me home the other night." She shrugged. "And I could be wrong, too. As I said, it might be nothing more than my fertile imagination. Or the fact that the first line translated talks about a curse if the papyrus falls into the wrong hands."

What if it wasn't? *Was* she in danger?

"The federal police don't deal in curses. We deal in cold, hard facts, ma'am. Like the fact that you've been followed," Agent Banks chimed in.

Emily glared at him. "No, I didn't say I *had* been followed. I just felt...maybe? And I sure as hell don't think that's enough to stick me with a bodyguard. The last thing I want is a man in my house. I wouldn't know what to do with him."

Agent Banks wouldn't look at her. Instead, he struggled to loosen the expensive tie that went with his equally expensive black suit. His mouth twitched and his serious façade dissolved as he started to cough.

Emily was sure she heard a snigger of laughter mixed in with the harsh convulsions the agent did little to control. She frowned, casting her mind back over what she'd said. A groan surfaced, but she bit it off before it passed her lips. God, she was at it again, sticking her foot in her mouth as soon as she opened it. Why didn't she think before she spoke? No doubt the guy had turned her simple little sentence into something with a sexual connotation, even if she *hadn't* meant it that way.

With a frustrated sigh, she flicked her hair back over her shoulder. What was with these men? They tell her something so outrageous and sit there trying not to laugh?

But maybe it isn't totally outrageous. A feeling of unease slithered through her mind. Last night, she could have sworn someone was outside her front door. She'd heard a noise, as if somebody had bumped against one of the hanging pots on the front porch. By the time she'd reached the door, Ria, her feline housemate, was throwing herself against the timber barricade, hissing and scratching.

Ria was better than any watchdog so Emily had heeded her warning. She'd decided not to open the door and find out if anyone was there. Instead, she'd huddled to one side so she wouldn't be seen through the glass panels in the door, ear against the woodwork, listening for any movement. When she'd checked in the light of day, there was nothing to suggest that anyone had been there. She'd put it down to Ria responding to another cat or even a dog wandering onto her porch. Yet now, she felt as if the whole world had gone mad, or at least her little part of it. This discovery was hers, the translation *her* job to perform. She just wished they'd all let her get on with it."

"Why would anyone want to harm a professor of Egyptology? It's only a little scrap of parchment, for heaven's sake." Pushing her glasses back up her nose, she turned toward Professor Williams, the Dean of the University of Sydney. "I can't understand why you felt the need to tell the federal government about this anyway. Or why you didn't wait until I at least had the thing translated."

Professor Williams wiped the grin off his face before he answered her. "Emily, if what you say is correct, this is an important discovery. I had no choice in the matter. Any major research project affecting the security of the nation has to be reported."

"The security of the nation? You're kidding, right?" She wanted to laugh, but the serious expressions on both agents' faces stopped her. "This is ridiculous." She was seriously tempted to stamp her foot in frustration. "From what I can gather, this is recipe for invisible paint. *Invisible paint?*" Now she did laugh. "I'll grant you the pharaohs did some remarkable things in their time—they were even doing brain surgery back then—but I don't believe they found a means of making themselves invisible. And even if it did work, I can't understand how it would be of use to the defense department. For crying out loud, it's probably some elaborate hoax."

"But the papyrus is real, isn't it?" Agent Banks cut in, now recovered from his coughing fit.

"Oh, it's real. I've had it carbon-dated, but until I've finished translating it, I'm not certain how important it is, beyond its antiquity value in the academic world."

"If it does happen to work, its value to the military would be astronomical. The applications for such a product would revolutionize military warfare for all time. It's an important find. And someone else seems to think it's important, too, and that's why you need a bodyguard."

Emily sighed as she shoved back her chair and surged to her feet. Heels clacking loud enough even the cheap carpet couldn't mute the sound, she strode across to the window overlooking the parking area.

"Damn it, I don't need a strange man cluttering up my little house," she muttered. "I like living alone, except for Ria, and who knows how long it will take to complete the translation?"

Having someone else there meant cooking meals at regular times. Not being able to slouch about the house in next to nothing when the heat became unbearable. Always having to present an image.

She sighed again and tapped her fingernail on the windowpane, the sound beating in time with the thoughts whizzing through her brain. A bad habit, one that annoyed her as much as it would anyone else listening. Like a pencil tapping rhythmically on a desk. She forced herself to stop and gazed out into the parking lot.

A solitary man stood near the bonnet of a sleek black car. As if he felt her watching, he turned to face the window, hands thrust into the pockets of his dark suit trousers, the fabric pulling tight across his well-muscled thighs.

The rest of him was just as impressive. He had to be at least six feet tall. Dark hair, perfectly cut. Emily grinned. The wind wouldn't dare to ruffle *that* well-groomed look. And his face... Oh, man!

Even from two floors up, with her slightly myopic gaze, his stunning good looks made the hormones go on a sudden rampage throughout her body. She deliberately tamped them down. "Nice. But too pretty."

She spun about when she heard the muffled sound of coughing from behind her. Marty Tomlins stood there, struggling to keep a straight face. She frowned at him in annoyance. "I can't see what's so damn hilarious, Agent Tomlins."

Tomlins straightened up, all sign of amusement wiped from his face. "Um, that's your bodyguard." He gestured to the man in the car park. "I think we should go down and you can meet him."

He didn't wait for her reply. Instead, he picked her purse up off the desk and thrust it into her hand. Then he took her arm and guided her out of the office. Agent Banks and Professor Williams followed closely behind.

Emily's mind was awhirl. "This whole thing is farcical. I don't need a bodyguard, certainly not one who'll be living with me twenty-four hours a day." She didn't want, or need, any man in her life, not for any reason. She'd had enough of handsome men like the one in the parking area.

One go around with a picture-book-perfect, so-called hero was enough. No way was she going to put herself in the same situation again.

They'd reached the steps leading down to the parking lot before she had the presence of mind to gather her scattered wits. She planted her feet, dragged her arm from the agent's hold and refused to go any further.

"Enough is enough. I do not need a bodyguard," she enunciated clearly. "I will not *have* a bodyguard. Now I know the dangers involved, I'll take more care. So if you'll excuse me, I have lectures to prepare." She turned to walk away, only to have Agent Banks grab her arm.

"Excuuuse me." She glared down at the hand holding her tight.

"You're not going anywhere, miss. This is not up for discussion. We're not taking any risks. You saw the state of your office here at the university. Totally trashed. *And* every file wiped from your computer, after someone copied it, no doubt. You'll take a bodyguard or you'll hand the parchment over to us."

A shiver traced its way down Emily's spine as she thought of the mess she'd found when she'd unlocked her office this morning. Someone had pulled the place apart. Campus security did rounds on all the offices between twelve and one each night, so it had to have happened some time after one. Thank God she hadn't worked late last night as she often did. She'd been home working on the translation instead. Funny, she hadn't even given the papyrus a thought when she'd realized someone had broken into her office.

She gave one final burst of token resistance, already knowing it was futile. "Look, guys, if I promise to take more care with my security, lock the papyrus away when I'm not working on it, will you lay off the bodyguard bit? I'll even consent to him being there during the day. Then I'll lock myself in after he goes. He doesn't need to stay full time." She tried for what she hoped was a winning smile. "It's only a birthday present, or at least a part of it, and probably a total hoax, knowing my friend."

"From what Professor Williams tells us, it's a lot more than that. It could be a very powerful weapon in the wrong hands. The scientists at the Department of Defense are eager to see the formula when you've finished translating those hieroglyphics, and with that end in mind, they're making certain you have no interruptions."

"But—"

"No buts. The discussion is ended," he stated emphatically, his face set in a serious cast.

Emily knew when she was beaten, but she didn't have to like it. "Did you have to choose such a good-looking agent for a bodyguard? Why couldn't I be assigned a woman? Handsome men have such ego problems. They all seem to think they're God's gift to the female race. They can't help but hit on a woman, for no other reason than to prove their virility. How can I work under those conditions?"

Damn, now she sounded as if she thought every man in her vicinity was out to score with her and that wasn't what she meant at all. Agent Tomlins looked like he was about to swallow his teeth. Emily frowned at him, daring him to laugh at her.

"It's all right, Miss Emily, Agent Farley is a professional. No way would he try to hit on a woman in the course of his duty. Besides, he's gay. You won't have any problems at all. It'll be like having a girlfriend staying with you."

He turned, bounded down the stairs and made his way over to the man in the parking area.

The sound of Tomlins' smothered laughter trailed after him. Emily shook her head in disgust. "Great. Now I don't have to worry about fighting off his advances. Instead, I'll have to fight for bathroom space. With a face like that, he probably spends all his time in front of the mirror."

Professor Williams patted her on the shoulder. "Now, Emily, it won't be that bad," he said in a patronizing, humor-the-little-woman tone of voice. "You're our top expert on Egyptology. If this is for real, it means a lot of money for the university. We need the translation on the papyrus as soon as possible. Agent Farley is there to see that it happens and to keep you safe, that's all."

"But I have lectures."

"It's been dealt with. Maxwell is going to take over your classes. All you have to do is concentrate on the translation."

Emily bit back another protest, knowing it was useless. "Terrific. Not only do I have crazy friends who send me Egyptian pots with ancient recipes in them, and a neurotic cat who goes into a fighting frenzy as soon as she sees it, now I get to spend time with Tinkerbell, the fairy prince."

༄༅

Nicholas straightened as Marty Tomlins approached him. His colleague was chuckling so hard he was in danger of falling flat on his face. What the hell was wrong with him? This was a serious assignment, nothing to laugh about. "What's with you, man?" he demanded as Marty reached him.

Marty clutched at his side and dragged in a deep breath before he answered. "Boy, you're going to love this one, Nick. I wish I could be there to see how you handle it."

Nicholas opened his mouth to ask what he was on about, but Marty cut across him.

"No time to explain now. Emily Payne is on her way over. Gotta ham it up, old boy. You've been undercover before. This time you'll really get the chance to try out your acting skills."

"What the hell...?"

Nicholas was not amused. Marty Tomlins was the biggest practical joker in the department, but Nicholas didn't have time for his tomfoolery right now. He should have been having a much-deserved break from work. In fact, he'd already left for his holiday destination when the boss had suddenly called him back and dumped this babysitting job on him. Christ, of all the jobs, this was the type he hated the most. Bloody babysitting. Now he simply wanted to get the assignment over and done with—minus Marty's jokes.

"Don't blame me. I had to do it," Marty said, a huge grin on his face.

"Do what, for crying out loud?" His voice snapped with annoyance. He fought to control it. That's what being an agent for the government was all about. Control. And Marty appeared to have lost it.

"The lady doesn't want a man in her house. Particularly a *pretty boy* agent. This is one time you won't be able to use your charm, mate. The lady thinks you're gay."

"I'm what?"

"Gay. And not as in funny ha ha. As in—"

"I know what gay is, Tomlins. Why the hell does Professor Payne think I'm gay?"

"It was the only way we could get her to agree to you staying in her house. You'll have to act all...you know, effeminate mannerisms and such." Marty roared with laughter as he leaned against the side of the nearest car, his hip cocked to one side and a limp-wristed hand waving in the air.

There was no time for any more discussion. Flanked by Agent Banks and Dean Williams, the woman walked right up to him.

So this is Professor Emily Payne. Nicholas didn't have to drop his gaze too far to make eye contact. She was only a few inches short of his six feet. Tall and willowy, just the way he liked them. But that's where any comparison with one of his numerous lady friends ended.

Emily Payne had jet-black hair that fell like a curtain about her shoulders. Black-framed glasses with pink tinted lens hid her eyes and a large portion of her face from view.

Nicholas was used to escorting women who dressed only in the latest fashions. All designer labels, of course. Emily Payne obviously didn't worry about fashion at all.

She was dressed in a bright pink floral blouse and an orange skirt that ended well below her knees. Both articles of clothing seemed to be a size too big, designed to hide any curves she might have. She reached up and removed her glasses. Her face looked smaller, more delicate, without them, but it was her eyes that held Nicholas's attention. Yellow topaz, like a precious piece of gold jewelry.

He shook his head. Now where the fuck had *that* come from? He was starting to sound like a freakin' poet. He took a deep breath. Okay, so her eyes were brown with golden highlights. Unusual, but not unheard of. And since when had the color of a woman's eyes mattered to him? It just wasn't important. Or it never had been—before he met Emily Payne. So why was it her gaze drew his like a magnet?

He forced himself to break eye contact and took in the picture as a whole. Forget the crazy color scheme. This woman looked like she belonged in one of the Egyptian murals in the museum. With her dark coloring and her unusual golden eyes with their slightly oriental slant, he'd bet odds she had Egyptian ancestry. Dress her in the right costume and she'd look like one of the pharaohs of ancient Egypt.

As he caught the glint in those golden eyes, a shudder swept through him. His lower body tightened with tension, his cock reminding him there was more to life than work. Shit, he needed to get himself in hand, instead of acting like a pre-pubescent kid caught in his first sexual fantasy.

The sound of Terry Banks clearing his throat broke through the sensual web holding him captive. It dragged him back from the X-rated scenario building in his mind. A wave of heat swept up his face as he held out his hand. "How do you do, Professor Payne. I'm Agent Nicholas Farley, your assigned bodyguard."

She wiped her palm down the side of her skirt before reaching out and grasping his hand. "I'm pleased to meet you, Agent Farley." She paused a moment before going on. "Well, I'm not really. Pleased to meet you, that is. Because I don't think I need a bodyguard."

She tilted her head to one side, lower lip caught between her teeth. A look of chagrin flashed across her face, bringing with it a tide of rosy color that highlighted her cheeks.

"Oh, dear, that was appallingly rude, wasn't it? Let's start over. I'm pleased to meet you, Agent Farley. Please call me Emily. If we're going to be living together, we shouldn't stand on formality, even if I don't want you in my home."

Nicholas grimaced as he heard Marty snigger behind his back. Crap, why did he have to get stuck with this assignment? The woman sounded like a kook, and a rude one at that.

Typical academic. Always living on a different plane than the rest of humanity. No practicality at all. He'd met a few so-called highly intelligent academics before. Absolutely brilliant in their fields, but take them out of their environment and dump 'em in the real world, and they were blithering idiots. Now why did he have the feeling Emily Payne fell into the same bracket? Great at her job and a total ditz the rest of the time. Didn't she know how important this discovery was? Although why it should matter to him, he couldn't fathom. It was, after all, nothing but another job.

Nicholas made himself concentrate as Emily started speaking again.

"I'm sorry how that came out, Agent Farley, but I really don't see the need for a bodyguard. I'm sure I'm smart enough to look after my own security. And a man in my home is really of no use at all."

"Now, Emily, you need a man there to protect you," Professor Williams spluttered.

Marty and Terry dissolved into unrestrained laughter again, any pretense at seriousness conspicuous by its absence. Even Nicholas found it difficult to keep a straight face.

Emily Payne directed a fierce scowl at the four men. It was enough to make them launch into a renewed round of hilarity. Nicholas tried for a professional face, but his lips had a tendency to twitch. Hell, the woman had an unfortunate habit of sticking her foot in her mouth. He couldn't wait to see what she came out with next.

"Damn, why do I do this?" she muttered. "How can I be such an intellect in the archaeology field and come over as a dumb bunny as soon as I meet a presentable man? Although this one's not. A man, that is. Well, he is, but not straight."

Nicholas strained to hear what she was saying, but her voice was so low he was having trouble.

"Hmm, maybe it won't be too bad. I won't have to worry about presenting an image. It doesn't matter with Agent Farley. Because he's gay."

Huh? "Ah, Ms. Payne, what—"

"Oh, stop it, Emily. You're driving yourself crazy."

"I'm sorry, did you say something, Professor?" Nicholas shook his head. *The woman really is an idiot. She even talks to herself.*

Crazy or not, she was a knockout, even in those dreadful clothes. She had the most exquisite and open face he'd ever seen, her every expression showing in her unusual cat-like eyes. If he didn't miss his guess, she was seriously pissed off, both at the situation and the four men standing in front of her.

The women he knew buried everything deep inside, allowing a man to see only what they wanted him to see. This woman intrigued him. She also had the most kissable lips he'd ever seen.

And he was supposed to act like he was gay?

"Oh, for crying out loud," Marty interrupted. "How about you let me make the introductions all over again? Emily, this is Nicholas. Nicholas, Emily. Now will you two get on with it? Who knows what could happen with you guys out here in plain view?"

Nicholas frowned. Marty was right. Standing out in the open in an unprotected parking lot went against everything he'd ever been taught. He'd better get his act together.

"Right. Let's get this show on the road," he said in his official, no-nonsense voice. He guided Emily around to the far side of his car. Taking the keys from his pocket, he bent down to unlock the passenger door.

Emily took a brief moment to stare at the sleek line of the shiny black BMW. *Hmm, nice, if that's what turned you on.* When Nicholas opened the door, she climbed into the bucket seat and reached out to grab the door handle.

"Don't slam..."

Too late. Emily had already sequestered herself inside with considerable force.

"...the door," he finished off, accompanied by the laughter of the other two agents. He rounded the vehicle and seated himself behind the steering wheel, glaring across at her.

"Well, excuuuse me, but it's only a car." Emily couldn't understand what the problem was.

As if to drive the point home, Nicholas eased the driver's door gently shut. Then he ignored her as he turned the ignition on and gunned the engine of the sporty car before driving out of the parking area and heading toward the rear entrance to the university grounds.

Emily, about to apologize, chose to remain silent so he could concentrate on his driving. It wasn't until they were almost at Paddington that she spoke. "I really am sorry about slamming the door, but it *is* only a car."

"It's more than that. It's the culmination of years of saving. I've always wanted to own a BMW."

Emily bit her lip. Damn, she really wanted to say it, but maybe she should shut her mouth in this instance. Nicholas was uptight enough already. Ah, crap, what the hell? "You know, there's a certain section of the psychology field that thinks a man's car is nothing more than a phallic symbol. An extension of... Well, his own...shortcomings, I guess you could say. Perhaps that's so in your case."

She settled deeper into the supple leather of the bucket seat. "Do you think it's got something to do with your being gay? When did you come out? Perhaps you're not comfortable yet with the idea that everyone knows. You shouldn't let what people think get to you."

There was a sudden spluttering from the man sitting beside her. She turned her head to look at him, but his face was devoid of expression.

"My sexual proclivity is not up for discussion," he spat out.

"I was only trying to be helpful."

Emily mentally shrugged. Boy, he sure was touchy. Living with this man for any length of time could prove a problem. Particularly if he took exception to every comment she made.

She glanced out the window and realized they were almost home. Traveling in style sure beat taking public transport. She breathed in the scent of expensive leather and something else. An elusive, spicy scent teased her senses. Aftershave, emanating from Nicholas.

The man not only looks good. He smells good, too. Wonder if he tastes as good. Heat crawled through her body at the thought. A delicious shiver feathered down her spine.

Emily, get real, she remonstrated with herself. *The man is gay. He is not up for grabs, and don't forget, you do not want a man in your life.*

"Even so, it's a damn shame. What a waste," she murmured.

"Excuse me?"

Crap, I'm doing it again, talking to myself. Nicholas was going to think she was a total nut job. "Nothing. Thinking out loud here. Oh, this is my street. I live—"

"Number Five Paddington Street. I already know."

Nicholas guided the car down the narrow street lined with huge Plane trees. All the buildings were restored Victorian terrace houses. It was almost as if he'd stepped back in time. The only thing marring the picture were the modern vehicles parked along the sides of the street. He drew the car to a halt in front of number five.

The outside of the house was a soft cream shade, a match for its neighbors. The iron lacework edging the roofline of both first and second floors was stark white, as was the front fence and balcony rail.

The patina of age had darkened the polished timber door, but it was the elaborate stained-glass panels in the door that held Nicholas's attention. They had to be original, as old as the door. Bright splashes of color in the hanging planters broke up the starkness of the muted scheme. It all added up to an authentic picture of an era long gone.

"Did you do the work yourself?" He gestured to the front of the house as he climbed out of the car.

"Except for the kitchen, it was fully restored when I bought it. This was my present to myself when I received tenure from the university."

Emily made a point of gently closing the car door. Nicholas grinned as he retrieved an overnight bag from the trunk and followed Emily to the front entrance.

"Sorry I don't have a garage, but don't worry, there hasn't been a car theft from here in quite a while."

Nicholas grimaced, praying his baby would be safe. Well, there wasn't a damn thing he could do about it now. He mentally shrugged as he stepped inside, his eyes opening wide when he saw the interior of the house. It really was superb. Small, but authentically restored.

The walls in the hallway were all tongue-in-groove timber painted in a pale pastel shade. A picture rail ran along the top of the wall, supporting what looked like original oil paintings of early Australia. The floor was timber, polished to a high sheen, as was the staircase leading to the upper level. Throw rugs spread around gave it all a familiar, warm feeling.

He followed Emily into the living room opening off the central hallway. This room, too, was furnished in keeping with the period of the house. Heavy, dark-stained pieces that blended in perfectly, although the couch didn't look any too comfortable. He sure hoped she had a spare bedroom.

"Kitchen's on the other side of the hallway." Emily dropped her purse and glasses on the coffee table. "It may look antiquated, but it has all the mod cons. The builder designed them to fit in with the décor."

She moved back into the hallway. "Bring your bag and I'll show you where you're sleeping."

Nicholas trailed in Emily's wake as they ascended the stairs. Suddenly, a thought hit him. Shit, some bodyguard he was. He should have gone first to make certain no one else was in the house.

Although come to think of it, this wasn't so bad. He had a perfect view of Emily's cute ass. The oversize skirt may hide her curves when she was standing still, but walking up stairs presented quite a different picture.

Stop it, Nicholas, he warned himself. *The lady is nothing but an assignment. Besides that, she thinks you're gay. Get your mind back on the job.*

"Ah, maybe you should let me go first." He made a valiant effort to focus only on the case.

"Why? I know my way around. After all, I live here."

He shook his head. The woman was going to drive him crazy. "I really should check the premises out first. Someone could have tried to break in here as well as at the university."

"Oh?"

She appeared to take a moment to think about it before shaking her head.

"No, we would have seen some evidence when we came in. The front door was still locked, so it's okay. Although they wouldn't need to break in. I have to leave the back door unlocked all the time. The lock is—"

"You what?" he interrupted.

He dropped his bag and raced down the stairs, heading for the kitchen and the back door. He couldn't believe what he'd heard. In this day and age, to leave a door unlocked was inviting trouble. She may as well hand out engraved invitations to all the local burglars.

He found the back door as she'd said.

Unlocked.

What made it worse was the cat flap in the bottom big enough for a small man to climb through. Was the woman totally flaky? Did she have no thought for her own safety?

Nicholas opened the door and stepped through into a small cottage garden. A profusion of flowers filled the area. There was no order, one color blending into another. A hotchpotch of vibrant splashes. A veritable rainbow. A bit like Emily herself.

It was the large tree branches hanging over the high fence that gave him cause for concern. Anyone determined to get in wouldn't need a ladder. All they had to do was climb the nearest tree.

Well, no point worrying about it now. He doubted very much Emily would let him cut down any of the overhanging limbs. He'd have to make certain he kept the door locked.

He spotted the sensor lights as he turned to re-enter the house. At least he'd have some warning if anyone came over the fence. After he'd locked the door and secured the cat flap, he took the stairs two at a time and joined Emily. "Shall we finish the guided tour, Professor?"

Emily remained silent, her attention blatantly fixed on his lower body, her lip caught between her teeth. A flush stained her cheeks and if he didn't miss his guess, given the slight smile teasing at the corners of her mouth, raunchy thoughts filled her mind.

The blood immediately left his head and rushed south, his cock rising to the occasion and letting him know it was taking notice. Crap, he'd be in deep trouble here if he didn't get his mind—and hers if he was reading her right—off the sexual and onto the mundane.

"Um, Emily, the room. Remember? I still need a bed for the night." *Great, why did I have to mention bed?*

Emily gave him one last lingering look before she spun about and strutted down the hallway.

"There are only the two bedrooms and a bathroom up here and this bedroom I've turned into my office." She paused at the entrance to a small room.

Nicholas glanced inside. The room was totally disorganized, papers lying everywhere. On the desk. On top of the computer. All over the floor. Had someone broken in here as well? Or was this the way she normally worked?

Suddenly, he heard it. A slight noise. A rustle. A scratchy sound like someone dragging something along the wooden floor. And it was coming from the other side of the large desk.

He motioned to Emily to be quiet, slid his hand under the back of his jacket and drew the standard issue Glock 17 from the pancake holster attached to his belt. All his protective instincts rose to the fore. A rush of adrenaline invaded his system. It sharpened his senses and focused his mind. Cautious, breath held, he crept toward the end of the desk.

"That's Ria, my cat. You won't need the gun. She's really very sweet. Well, most of the time."

When Emily stepped up behind him and popped her head around his arm, Nicholas jerked in reaction. Taking a deep breath, he loosened his grip on his weapon and stared.

A jet-black cat with the most amazing yellow eyes squatted among broken shards of pottery. An errant thought, that the cat was very like her mistress, flitted though his mind. He quickly dismissed it as he realized how silly he must look, standing there holding a gun on a cat. He tucked the weapon away, bent down and extended his hand.

"Looks like she's knocked a pot off your desk." He tried to pick up a piece of the broken pottery, only to have the cat snake out a paw, claws extended, and smack him on the wrist. Blood welled immediately from the scratch. A loud hiss issued from the animal's mouth. Nicholas glared at the cat, but the bloody thing simply bared its teeth at him, its mouth curled back in what looked like a sneer.

"Oh, she knocked that off a few weeks ago. That's how I found the papyrus. A friend on an archaeological dig in Egypt sent the pot to me. The papyrus was hidden inside."

"Why haven't you picked the broken bits up? If you walk on them with bare feet, you'll cut yourself to pieces."

"Ria won't let me. For some reason she took an instant dislike to the pot. I've never seen her hiss at anything like that before. It's a marriage pot. History shows the ancient Egyptians filled them with scented massage oils used to anoint the bride in a mating ceremony. The old folklore says if you introduce one of those into your household, your days are numbered, you'll soon be mated for life."

Emily chuckled. "Maybe Ria is worried I'll get hitched and won't have time for her. Cats are very territorial. She knocked the pot flying as soon as I set it on the desk. Now she won't let me touch it."

"Why not clean it up when she's out in the garden?"

She shrugged. "Why bother? It'll only upset Ria. If she wants to stand guard over a busted pot, who am I to say she shouldn't? It's lucky she didn't rip the papyrus to shreds."

Nicholas closed his eyes, shook his head and prayed for patience. "Where's the papyrus now? Somewhere safe, I hope?"

"Oh, perfectly safe." Emily reached inside the front of her shirt and extracted a folded plastic sleeve containing the ancient scrap of writing material from her bra. "No one would think of looking for it here."

He groaned. No one but this woman would hide a priceless object in her underwear.

"Nicholas, are you all right? You've gone quite red in the face. Perhaps I should show you where you're sleeping. Maybe you need to have a lie-down."

She led the way into the other bedroom. A large four-poster bed dominated the room, flanked by two small bedside tables. A lacy cover and embroidered throw cushions, as well as the lace curtains hanging from the canopy of the bed, turned the whole room into a scene for seduction.

French doors framed by the same lacy fabric opened out onto a covered balcony. A cheval mirror stood to one side and an antique rocking chair, piled high with fluffy cushions, held pride of place near the open doors.

Open?

He ran his hand through his hair. Lord, she'd be the death of him. She'd gone out and left these unlocked, too. Shaking his head in disbelief, he turned again to face the bed.

"Ah, Emily, there's only one bed. Where am I supposed to sleep?"

Emily beamed at him. "Oh, I've thought about that. If you'd been a man, I mean a straight man, we'd have a problem. As it is, we don't have to worry."

"What do you mean by that?" A feeling of dread settled inside him.

"Well, you're too big for my little couch and I know for a fact I can't sleep on it. Seeing as how you're...you know...gay, I thought we could both share the room. It'll be like having a sleep-over."

Oh, for fuck's sake, she expects me to sleep with her? He found himself wildly attracted to the biggest kook he'd ever met and now he had to sleep with her?

With a silent curse, he struggled to damp down the surge of anticipation rippling through his body. He couldn't believe how hard it was to discipline himself, to clear his mind of the vivid mental pictures of himself and the crazy professor cuddled up together in that bed. Come to think of it, that wasn't the only thing that was hard.

He groaned at life's little irony. Here he was, with a woman who looked like an Egyptian goddess and he was supposed to pretend she didn't turn him on. Nicholas Farley, the heartthrob of the agency, the man who never had a problem with women. A man for whom self-control had never been an issue. And now his body was betraying him and he couldn't do a damn thing about it.

He was supposed to be gay.

Chapter Two

Nicholas stood in the middle of the room and stared at the bed as a tidal wave of panic washed over him, threatening to drown him in its wake. He had a strong feeling he shouldn't do this, at least not if he wanted to keep his peace of mind.

"Maybe I should...I could, ah, I could sleep on the floor," he muttered, his command of the English language failing him for once.

She frowned at him. "Um, that's actually what I meant when I said we could share the room."

A shaft of disappointment sliced its way through Nicholas. For a moment, he felt as if someone had deprived him of his favorite toy. He shook his head. What the hell was wrong with him? *Professionalism*, he reminded himself. *Professionalism!*

"And I have just the thing. One of those blow-up mattress jobs."

Huh? Damn, he needed to pay attention here. "You mean an airbed?"

Emily hustled over to the wardrobe in the corner of the room and yanked the doors open. Then she rummaged around in the bottom and Nicholas was treated to the curvy shape of her ass as her skirt pulled tight. He gritted his teeth as testosterone flooded his system. Shit, he was in trouble.

"Here you go. Catch."

He looked up to see a folded square of vinyl sailing through the air toward him. Only his quick reflexes prevented the thing from smacking him in the face.

"I haven't used it for a while and I have no idea where the foot pump is, but it shouldn't take long to blow it up by mouth. I'll get some linen out for it later."

Nicholas shook his head. The woman had to be crazy. He'd be here all night. Then he ceased to worry about it. He was working too hard at keeping his body under control.

His gaze followed her as she strode over to a polished set of drawers. After retrieving a handful of fresh clothing, she came back to the bed and stood right in front of him. She tossed the clothing on the end of the bed and before he could react, reached up and laid the back of her hand on his forehead.

"Are you sure you don't want to lie down, Nicholas? You don't seem to have a temperature, but you've got the strangest look on your face."

"No, I'm fine."

"Perhaps you've got a headache. I could get you a couple of painkillers." She took his arm, guided him over to the bed and urged him to sit down. "You stay here and I'll be right back." She started to turn away, but he grabbed her hand.

"I don't have a headache. I don't feel sick. I really am all right, Emily."

"Oh? Okay then. Well, I'm going to change into something more comfortable before I get us some lunch. How about you spread that air mattress out down there near the French doors and blow it up?"

Nicholas sat there dumbfounded for a few minutes. Holy shit, he'd been manipulated by an expert. Nicholas Farley, highly trained special agent, and he'd allowed this crazy woman to lead him around like a child.

Shock rocketed through him when Emily casually unzipped her skirt. She was undressing in front of him? He couldn't believe it. She really did buy this gay nonsense.

"Ah-humm."

He shook his head as Emily cleared her throat.

"The airbed, Nicholas! And keep your back turned while I change, please."

Heat scorched Nicholas's cheeks. Shit, he was blushing like a schoolboy caught peeking in the girls' locker room. Dragging his gaze from where she clutched the unzipped skirt about her waist, he hastily dropped to his knees and spread the airbed out where she'd indicated.

A flicker of movement in the corner of his eye snagged his attention. The valve of the mattress in his mouth, ready for the first puff of air, he slid his gaze sideways. The free-standing cheval mirror on the opposite side of the French doors afforded him a perfect picture of Emily as she released her hold on her skirt.

The tapering length of her legs drew his interest. Her blouse fell almost to the top of her legs. All he could see of her panties was a tiny vee of ivory lace at the apex of her thighs. And, God help him, he couldn't keep his eyes off it.

With a superhuman effort, he averted his eyes and swallowed the lump lodged in the back of his throat. He'd have a major problem if he kept staring. He could already feel his body reacting to the enticing sight of Emily's legs, blood pumping down to pool in his groin.

He sat back on his heels and dropped his hands into his lap to hide his rising erection. Not that it would do much good if he didn't get himself under control. And quick.

Dammit, he couldn't help himself. He had to look. What red-blooded male could turn away when an attractive woman stripped in front of him? It was a poor justification, and it wasn't exactly in front of him, but the best he could come up with at short notice.

In between each tortured breath into the airbed, he watched as Emily struggled into a skin-tight pair of bright yellow leggings. When she'd settled them about her waist, she started to undo the buttons of her blouse. He felt like a pervert, but he didn't have the strength to close his eyes or turn his head away.

He tracked her movements from one button to the next. It was like unwrapping Christmas presents, waiting for the final piece of paper to fall to reveal the treasure within.

As the blouse parted and Emily shrugged it off her shoulders, he almost let loose with a deep groan. Who would have thought it? The woman dressed in old-fashioned clothes, but underneath the outer covering, it was a different matter.

The lady was a total paradox. If such a thing were possible, he was sure his eyes would have fallen out of his head. The professor obviously went in for sexy underwear.

A scrap of red fabric confined her breasts. There wasn't much of it. Just enough to cup and lift the most perfect breasts he'd ever seen. Not too large. Not too small. A perfect fit. His fingers twitched to reach out and fill his hands with them.

The bra was one of those half-cup things, barely covering her nipples. Although it wouldn't have mattered if it had been a neck-to-knee job. The fabric was so sheer he could clearly see the dark areolas surrounding her nipples.

I've died and gone to heaven. Nicholas shook the thought away and struggled to control his rising libido. Who did she think he was—Superman?

His eyes opened wide with shock when Emily reached behind her back to release the clasp on the bra. He had to do something, before he totally disgraced himself. His cock was already so damn hard, it was a wonder he didn't shoot his load then and there. He needed to get out of the room for a bit. He jumped to his feet and backed toward the bed.

"Maybe I should change out of this suit," he mumbled as he hefted his overnight bag up from the floor.

He kept his head turned as he threw the bag on the bed, almost knocking a glass bowl off the bedside table. He grabbed it before it could fall. Foil-wrapped packets flew out of the bowl and settled on the surface like a drift of silver snowflakes, with the odd flash of vivid color thrown in for effect.

Silently cursing his clumsiness, Nicholas grabbed the packets up one by one and dropped them back into the container. As he replaced the last of them, his brain suddenly registered what they were.

The woman kept a bowl of condoms beside her bed, within easy reach. *A whole bowl?* Hell, he'd heard of keeping a box in the drawer, but a bowl full of the suckers? There must be at least four dozen there. Talk about being prepared.

He shook his head in disbelief and turned to his bag, extracting jeans and a tee shirt from the jumbled contents. An object flew over his shoulder and landed on the bed in front of him. He gulped and almost forgot to breathe.

A sexy, super-sheer red bra.

He had a sudden, inexplicable desire to reach out and touch. To feel the heat of her body on the filmy fabric. His hands trembled, so bad was the need.

Dragging in a sharp breath, he struggled to get himself under control. At this rate, he'd end up a basket case. He'd be no use at all if someone tried to break in and steal the papyrus.

Somehow, he'd have to ignore Emily and his own raging testosterone and focus on the fact that this was nothing but a job.

Emily stared at Nicholas as she settled the tee shirt about her hips. He was hunched over the bed, pulling clothing from his overnight bag.

A blanket of heat crawled up her face. She couldn't believe she'd casually removed her clothes with Nicholas in the room. Thank God he'd kept his back to her. Even so, she still felt a bit weird. It was just like having a girlfriend come to stay, she excused herself. Funny, she'd never felt this aware when her friend Miranda stayed over.

She studied the set of Nicholas's shoulders. He seemed...tense, his body held stiffly as if it would shatter if he so much as moved a muscle. Perhaps he wasn't used to sharing living space with another person. She hadn't thought to ask whether he was in a relationship.

Maybe he was embarrassed at the idea of a woman changing her clothes. After all, it was something he probably wasn't used to. Perhaps she'd better be a bit more considerate of his feelings in future. Underneath that no-nonsense demeanor, he seemed a nice man. The problem was, she was used to living on her own.

"Nicholas, are you in a relationship? Perhaps there's someone you'd like to call to let them know where you are."

He turned to face her. "No, there's no one at the moment. The Agency knows where I am if anyone wants to contact me." A pained expression flitted across his face. "Ah, Emily, do you really mean to wear that?"

"What wrong with it? It's comfortable. I don't have to dress up when I'm at home."

"It's...well, the tee shirt's emerald green. With yellow leggings? The colors are great with your dark hair and fair skin, but together?"

"Oh, is that all? It's okay, I'm color-blind. That's why I wear glasses. The special tint on the lens is supposed to help correct the problem. I have contacts as well, but because they hurt my eyes, I don't wear them very often. I don't bother too much at home, but I do usually try and make an effort when I go to work."

She paused, a grin curving her lips. "Although I kind of ran out of time this morning and dressed in a rush. It wasn't until I got to work I realized I'd mixed bright pink with vivid orange."

She whirled toward the door of the bedroom. "Not that anyone takes any notice of me anyway. They're used to the fact that I'm a total screw-up in the real world, even if I am considered the top of my field here in Sydney." She dragged in a deep breath. "Enough of this. I'm hungry. How about you get changed and meet me down in the kitchen? I'll rustle up something to eat."

ꕥ

Emily stood at the kitchen sink washing the lettuce to go with the salad she was preparing. The job was mechanical, requiring little thought. She allowed her gaze to sweep over the explosion of color in her back garden. This was one thing she loved about her little kitchen—she could stand here working and still observe the outside world. It was the main reason she never pulled the curtains across the large window above the sink. And what did it matter if she didn't see the colors as nature meant them to be? It was still a delight for the senses.

The sound of high-pitched whining dragged her back to the present. Ria slunk about the kitchen, complaining loud enough to let the whole world know she was unhappy with her lot in life.

Tail held high, she twisted about Emily's legs, stopping every so often to vocalize her displeasure. When Emily didn't respond immediately, Ria swiped at the bright, yellow-clad leg nearest her with her front paw.

"Hey, enough of that. You can smell the salmon, can't you? If you hang on a moment, I'll give you some."

Emily wiped her hands on a paper towel and reached down to give Ria a pat. The cat took a swing at her hand, not interested in petting. "Ria, you really have an attitude problem. Stop being so impatient."

She scraped some of the salmon she'd planned for lunch onto an old saucer and placed it on the floor in the corner. The cat wandered over, sniffed at the offering and promptly ignored it, stalking about the room again. Finally, she settled in front of the back door, loudly proclaiming her annoyance.

"You're a nuisance, Ria. What on earth is wrong with you?"

From past experience, she knew the cat wouldn't stop until Emily had righted whatever was wrong. When she joined Ria at the back door, she realized what the problem was. Nicholas had not only locked the back door, he'd secured the cat flap as well. No wonder poor Ria was throwing a fit.

She unlocked the flap from inside, but that only allowed it to swing in one direction. She'd also have to unbolt it from outside. She cursed under her breath as she struggled with the back door.

There was a perfectly good reason she never locked this door. She always had difficulty dealing with the stubborn thing and today was no exception. Plus, this was a good area. She'd never heard of any house break-ins ever happening. She'd always felt safe here. Although in the light of what had transpired at the university, she probably needed to give that more thought.

The door finally came open with a whoosh and Emily stumbled backward, the cat darting between her legs. Within minutes, Ria had disappeared among the flowers. After taking a quick look around the yard to check she was alone, Emily leaned against the door jam and enjoyed the moment, breathing in the heady scent of the flowering jasmine climbing over the side fence.

Suddenly, she heard a noise that didn't belong in her peaceful garden. Was that a man's voice? Her neighbors on both sides were away on holidays, so it couldn't be coming from there.

Tension gripped her as she slowly allowed her gaze to track across the garden. Nothing. She was about to turn away when she spotted movement in one of the overhanging branches. Ria stood beneath the branch, her back arched, hissing loudly. There was someone in the tree. Ria would never act that way unless there was danger.

Emily backed up until she reached the door into the hallway, tiptoeing over to the bottom of the staircase. "Nicholas," she whispered as loud as she dared. "*Nicholas.*"

"Is lunch ready? I'll be there in a moment. I need to hang this suit up."

"Shh. There's someone in the tree in my garden," Emily whispered, her heart pounding hard in her chest.

Nicholas threw his suit over the railing. In one smooth movement, he bent down, pulled up the leg of his jeans and palmed the small handgun resting in the holster strapped to his leg a few inches above his ankle. As he bounded down the stairs two at a time, he muttered, "Why didn't you say so?"

"I just did." Emily jumped out of the way as he raced for the kitchen and the open door. By the time she reached the garden, Nicholas was already at the back fence.

He launched himself at the lowest branch. When he had a firm hold, he braced his feet on the timber fence and hauled himself up into the tree.

Emily couldn't help but admire the rippling muscles perfectly delineated by the tight-fitting tee shirt. Despite the seriousness of the situation she had to smile. The rear view was as good as the front. *Oh yeah, the man obviously works out.*

She shook her head at the sheer waste of a good man and joined Ria under the tree. She couldn't see Nicholas, but she heard him. And she also heard the car that took off at the back of her property. It looked like the danger was over.

Nicholas cursed fluently as the vehicle, driven at high speed, disappeared down the lane. It had all happened so quickly, he hadn't had a chance to get a look at the color and make, let alone the license number. He crawled back along the branch and lowered himself down beside Emily. Bending, he holstered the gun, folding the leg of his jeans down to hide it.

"You could have saved yourself some bother and used the gate," Emily said.

Nicholas closed his eyes and counted silently to ten. By all that was holy, how the hell had he managed to get assigned to this job?

"Where's the gate? I didn't see one when I was out here earlier." He made a determined effort to keep his temper in check.

Emily squinted at him, eyes narrowed against the sun. “Are you angry? Don’t feel bad he got away. He was obviously too fast for you.”

“Where’s the gate, Emily?” He gritted his teeth and did the counting thing again. At the rate he was going, he’d be up to a hundred in no time flat.

She pointed to the corner of the yard where a tangle of bushes obscured the top of the fence. Now he knew where it was, Nicholas could make out some of the outline of the timber gate. “I hope the gate is locked, Emily.”

“Well, it has got a padlock on it.” She shrugged.

“Good.”

“But I never close it. I don’t know where the key is if I want to unlock it again, although I’ve never had need of it the whole time I’ve been here.”

Nicholas bit down on his bottom lip. He wanted to pick Emily up and shake her for being so cavalier about her personal safety. Not that he thought it would do much good. Emily appeared to live in a little world of her own making and ordinary everyday events seemed to pass her by. Nothing he said would make a scrap of difference. Besides, he had to live with the woman for the moment. It wouldn’t do to get her angry with him. He needed her in the right frame of mind to translate the papyrus.

In an effort to replace frustration with action, he clambered through the bushes until he reached the gate. Rust had turned the padlock a burnt orange color, but with brute force he managed to lock it. Emily would just have to buy a new lock after all this was over. He backed out of the bushes, muttering to himself as branches caught at his hair and scratched his hands.

Once free of the clinging foliage, he grabbed Emily by the arm and marched her inside, the cat strutting regally behind. Still silent, he waited until Ria was inside before bolting the cat flap and locking the back door. Finally, he turned to face Emily, his hands planted on his hips.

"Why did you open the back door?"

"Huh?" She shook her head, as if trying to focus on his words.

"The door, Emily. Why did you open it?"

"Ria needed to go out. What else was I supposed to do?" She held up her hand as he opened his mouth to speak. "I'm not totally stupid. I did check first to make certain there was no one there. And there wasn't when I first opened the door."

"You should have called me first. How am I going to protect you if you keep flouting all the rules?"

"I didn't know there were any rules. How could I? I'm not used to having a bodyguard."

"There *are* rules. I make them, you obey them. Is that clear? If I lock a door, it stays locked."

"Fine. But you get to take the cat out every time she needs to go."

"Can't you put a litter tray in the laundry for her?"

"She doesn't like it. Besides, I don't have any kitty litter in the house."

"We'll get some tomorrow. In the meantime, I'll see to the cat."

Emily smiled to herself. Nicholas didn't know what he was letting himself in for. Ria wouldn't take kindly to change in her routine. *And* she didn't particularly like men. She was a real pain in the ass when she wanted to be. With a hastily suppressed snigger, she returned to the bench to finish making lunch.

She knew Nicholas was angry with her, and given he was responsible for her safety, he had a right to be. She should apologize for being such a flake at times, but all she could focus on was the picture he made standing there in his tight jeans and tee shirt. Her mouth watered and hormones kicked into overdrive. She'd never been so instantaneously attracted to a man before. Without doing anything at all, this one seemed to push all the right buttons.

Need flashed through her body. Her breasts felt swollen, the nipples supersensitive as they brushed against the fabric of her tee shirt. Tension coiled tight in her belly, highlighting the ache between her thighs. Without thinking, she rubbed her legs together, clenching her muscles, only to realize how wet she was. Crap, much more of this and she'd end up climaxing right in front of him. He hadn't touched her and she was as randy as an old rooster let free in a hen house.

Back off, Emily. The man is gay. He's not interested.

With a mammoth effort, she tried to concentrate on the mundane task of preparing a meal, but she was too conscious of Nicholas standing behind her watching her every move. Damn it, his being there made her all the more aware of the heated state of her...girlie bits.

A chuckle bubbled up. She couldn't believe she'd even thought that. She was cracking up through sheer sexual frustration. Her stomach was tied in knots. Her pussy was wet, her clit throbbed and she wanted to fuck the crap out of one Nicholas Farley. And she couldn't...because he was gay. Shit.

"Um, Nicholas, why don't you give me a hand? There's a loaf of bread in the oven. How about you slice it while I throw this salad together? Bread knife's in the top drawer."

Emily had always thought her kitchen was quite big. Now, with Nicholas prowling around, the walls seemed to shrink. She watched him out of the corner of her eye as he retrieved the knife and cutting board. She'd expected him to work on the other side of the room, but he threw her a bit when he placed the board on the bench beside her.

Her concentration was blown. She couldn't keep her eyes off the play of muscles as he sliced the bread. Such a simple action had suddenly become wildly enticing.

Her heartbeat accelerated, pulse pounding. With his every movement, Nicholas's aftershave wafted over her. It invaded her senses, creating a warmth of its own, burying the memory of the elusive scent deep in her consciousness. A fine sheen of sweat broke out on her face and the breath snagged in her throat.

"Ah, Emily?"

"Yes?"

"You can't actually wring lettuce out."

She looked down to find she'd twisted a lettuce leaf into a tight coil. Not wanting Nicholas to know how much he affected her, she fought to control the slight tremor in her hands. "It's okay. I'm going to rip the lettuce into pieces anyway. First, I have to make certain there's no excess water on it. Kinda makes the salad soggy otherwise." *Yeah, right.*

Putting action to words, she tore the salad vegetable into pieces and threw them into a bowl. She added quartered tomatoes, along with parsley sprigs, peppers and mushrooms. Giving it a drizzle of dressing and a quick toss, she placed it on the table then added the plate of salmon. "I'm not much of a cook." She grimaced. "This is the best thing I do at short notice. Plus the fact I haven't had time to go shopping."

"We'll see about getting groceries tomorrow." Nicholas slid the warm bread and a dish of butter onto the table and turned to pull a chair out for Emily.

A well-trained gentleman, she thought as she sat, dragging in a deep breath and catching another whiff of his spicy aftershave. It mingled with the aroma of hot bread, making her mouth water. *And* it wasn't just her taste buds reacting. Her libido was way out of control.

She made a valiant effort to rein in her racing hormones and push all erotic thoughts from her mind. Sex and salmon just didn't go together.

Nicholas began to speak and she had to concentrate on his words instead of the movement of his lips.

"Did you hear me, Emily? Who else but the Agency and Dean Williams knows about the papyrus?"

"Um, Maxwell was there when I told Dean Williams."

"Tell me about Maxwell."

"He's just another professor in the Archaeology Department. If you're thinking about the person in the tree, it wouldn't have been him."

Nicholas helped himself to a slice of bread, buttered it and lifted it to his mouth. She almost groaned as he bit down with perfect white teeth. Who would have thought eating would be such a sensual banquet?

"Emily, concentrate. Why wouldn't it be Maxwell?"

"For one thing, he's too conscious of his perfect image to mess it up by climbing a tree. Maybe Maxwell or Dean Williams mentioned the papyrus to someone else."

"Hmm, maybe. We'll have to check it out."

There was a hiatus of silence as they both concentrated on their meal. When she'd had enough, Emily pushed her plate away and rose from the table to make coffee.

"Just why *is* the government so interested in this? Is there something you're not telling me? Okay, it's worth a lot of money in terms of its archeological value, but as for being of use in the military field? Come on, that's a bit far-fetched, isn't it?"

"You were the one who said the translation mentioned something about invisibility. Whatever it was you told Dean Williams, it was enough he thought the government should know."

"So far all I've been able to glean is it's a recipe for paint. According to the hieroglyphics, anything painted with this substance becomes invisible." She paused, concentrating on pouring the coffee. She carried the cups across to the table and placed one in front of Nicholas before taking her seat.

"Imagine if it were true though. The pharaohs were supposed to have used cloaks of invisibility in their religious ceremonies. The local people thought they had magical powers, but the papyrus translation says they were using this special paint. Neat, huh? Although it's probably all a myth."

Nicholas leaned forward, his eyes lit with excitement. "If this works, it really *could* be used as a weapon. Imagine it. Tanks and armored personnel carriers all invisible. The enemy would never know when they're coming."

"Yes, they would. They'd hear the engines."

"Oh, Emily, stop being so pedantic. Use your imagination."

"If I have to imagine war, I'd prefer not to, thank you very much. I'll leave that to the government. I'll translate the papyrus. Then it's up to the army what happens with it."

Nicholas appeared lost in thought and Emily found herself focusing on his lips again. When those same lips began to move, it took a moment for her to register he was talking to her.

"It can't be a very involved formula."

"What makes you say that?"

"That scrap of papyrus you pulled from your...ah, your front... Well, it wasn't very big. There can't be much on it. How long will it take to finish the translation?"

"A few days. A week at most." She raised her eyebrows. "Who knows?"

"Why so long? I thought you were an expert."

"I am, but the hieroglyphs are so incredibly tiny, I have to use a magnifying glass to see them properly." She shrugged. "So it will take...as long as it takes."

He stood and circled the table, coming to a stop behind her chair. Emily shivered with delight at having him so near. She had to remind herself once again the man was gay. To top it off, she was supposed to be off men right now. It was an exercise in futility. Her brain wasn't listening.

"I'll clean this up and you go upstairs and get on with the translation."

Her whole body quivered as Nicholas's velvety voice washed over her. *Distance. I need to put some distance between us.*

Without a word, she rose from the table and left the kitchen.

Nicholas watched her scuttle out of the room as fast as those deliciously long legs of hers would carry her. And he could understand why.

He'd seen the awareness in her eyes. Felt the tension arcing between them. If he didn't miss his guess, Emily was reacting to him as a man, not as her personal bodyguard.

He wasn't much better. His body came alive each time he was near her. Even now, thinking about her, certain parts of his anatomy hardened with a desperate need.

Shit, he should have his head examined. Emily Payne was nothing more than an assignment. A body he was committed to guarding. A sneaky little voice in his brain painted a picture of that same body. Tall and slim, but curved in all the right places. The image of Emily in a sheer red bra flitted through his mind and lecherous thoughts suddenly gained precedence before he could stop them.

He grabbed the dishes from the table and stacked them in the sink. He needed something to take his mind off his... Well, suffice it to say, he needed to keep busy. He decided to wash the dishes by hand instead of using the dishwasher. If that didn't keep his mind, and his body, under control, nothing would.

The battle was lost when his thoughts immediately returned to Emily. "Okay," he murmured. "I can't stop thinking about her, so let's rationalize it. She's an attractive woman. An unusual lady. Any man would be taken with her. It's nothing more than testosterone. A natural function for a normal male."

The words sounded right, but he knew it wasn't true. He'd dated a lot of women. Street-smart, sophisticated women. Women who knew the score. And he'd never been more than mildly attracted to them.

Given the job he had, he couldn't afford emotional ties, which is why he'd never committed to any one person. The thought never even crossed his mind. Yet here he was, so twisted up in knots his gut ached. Along with the rest of him.

Emily wasn't like the other females he'd been involved with. She made him think of warm firesides on cold winter nights, lazy summer days spent lying together in her colorful cottage garden, finding pleasure in the simplest of household chores. Emily was permanence. Emily was *forever after, 'til death do us part*, something he felt he couldn't offer a woman. Too many relationships failed in his line of work.

"What the hell am I thinking? I've only just met the woman." He pulled the plug from the sink to allow the water to drain away. His movements were jerky, uncoordinated. Water splashed over the edge and down the front of his jeans, soaking through to his skin, molding the fabric to his semi-aroused body.

He'd been that way ever since meeting the good professor. He had to do something about it. He couldn't go around in this state for the next week.

And that was the other thing. Gay men weren't attracted to women, no matter how enticing they were. He'd have to put on a better act if he wanted to fool Emily. Ham it up a bit, as Marty said. He was a grown man, with strong self-discipline. He could do it.

After all, Emily Payne was nothing more than an assignment.

"Yeah, right," he muttered as he left the kitchen to check the locks on the downstairs windows. "Tell that to the Marines because this body isn't listening."

Chapter Three

Emily tapped her pursed lips with the tip of her index finger, her brow furrowed in concentration. With her other hand, she held the magnifying glass close to the scrap of papyrus and squinted down at the tiny etchings on the surface of the ancient communiqué. She absently rubbed her forehead, trying to ignore the nagging throb behind her eyes.

"Enough." Dropping the magnifying glass on the desk, she arched her back. Arms extended high above her head, she stretched first one way, then the other.

An idle glance through the open French doors showed it was dark outside. A perfumed breeze drifted in through the doorway and filled the room with the scent of jasmine and ginger flowers. The heavy, spicy smell of the ginger suddenly reminded her of Nicholas's aftershave.

"Now there's a man," she murmured as she propped her elbows on the desk and rested her chin on her clasped hands. "Well, he's not, but he is." She groaned. "Get real, Emily. Of course he's a man. He's just not straight. I've said it before, but I'll say it again. It's a crying shame. Such a waste."

She shook her head in disgust. The same thing had been happening all afternoon. The moment she took her focus off the translation, thoughts of her uninvited guest intruded, sending the blood pulsing through her body.

"I wonder if he is gay, or if he only thinks he is," she mused. "I mean, he doesn't act like he's gay. At least not like the few gay men I know."

"Talking to yourself, Ms. Payne?"

Emily jumped, elbows slipping off the desk, her chin almost coming to grief on the timber surface. Her heart pounded in her chest at the unexpected interruption.

"Don't do that. You scared me right out of my pants." She spun around to face him. Nicholas had closed his eyes and was clinging to the doorframe, as if it were the only thing keeping him upright.

"Hell, did you have to use a phrase like that?" he muttered.

"I'm sorry?"

"Nothing. I, ah, wanted... I called you from the top of the stairs, but you didn't respond. You must have been engrossed in those hieroglyphics."

Oh crap, I hope he didn't hear what I said. She really would have to stop vocalizing her thoughts.

"How's it going?"

"Well, another line done, but it's hard work. My back feels like it's breaking and my eyes are gritty from staring through the magnifying glass."

She watched him surreptitiously as he strode around the desk to reach the open doors. With a decisive snap, he closed them, shooting the bolt home. A final rattle of the handle and he turned to face her.

Emily dragged in a shaky breath as he moved closer. She couldn't take her eyes off the denim-clad thigh he rested against the side of the desk. Her gaze slid upward, taking in the full picture. A shaft of hot sexual energy arrowed through her body. *Oh dear, this won't do at all.*

"How about giving it a rest for now?" Nicholas suggested.

With her mind still firmly centered on the way Nicholas made her feel, it was difficult to focus on what he'd said. "Um, give what a rest?"

"The work. Take a break. You've been up here for hours. It's time for dinner anyway."

Dinner. Right. "I don't think... I'm not certain what I have in the house. Give me a few minutes to clear this up and I'll see what I can pull together."

"No need to worry. I found some steaks in the freezer. I only need to throw them under the broiler and dinner is ready to eat."

"Good gracious, a man who cooks. What more could a girl ask for?" *Someone who fancies women instead of men?*

She buried the unruly thought in the back of her mind and, picking up the papyrus with a pair of tweezers, placed it inside the crumpled plastic sleeve, adding her translation notes to it.

"Ah...you're not going to put that down your front again, are you?"

"Don't be silly. I'm not wearing a bra. It'd fall right through."

Nicholas found his gaze drawn to her unbound breasts, clearly outlined by the soft fabric of the well-washed emerald tee shirt. With a supreme effort, he averted his gaze and tried to concentrate on the subject at hand. "Where do you keep the papyrus when you're at home?"

"There's a safe downstairs. It'll be fine there overnight."

He couldn't believe it. The woman had the use of a perfectly good safe and she hid a priceless artifact in her bra?

Emily flicked off the desk lamp and left the office, Nicholas following her like a faithful puppy, his tongue almost hanging out as he fixated on the sway of her hips. She made her way down to the living room where a boston fern stood in the corner on a two-foot-high, polished timber planter stand. Trailing fern fronds cascaded from the center of the plant, draped over the side of the pot and reached almost to the floor. The splash of vibrant green stood out in stark relief against the pale walls, softening the formal design.

Laying the plastic sleeve on the floor, Emily dropped to her knees. Then she disappeared. Right underneath all that foliage. The plant began to move, the pot wobbling precariously. He reached out and slid his hands through the fronds until he could grasp the base and take the weight from her.

"Don't hurt her," she cried out. "She's very delicate."

Her? The plant had a gender? Nicholas was having trouble taking this in. He backed up a step and watched as Emily quickly shifted the planter stand and slid it back under the plant, lifting the fronds out of the way so he could place it down again.

It took him a minute before he could formulate a coherent thought. "Your plant is a she?"

"Of course. Her name is Abigail."

"Your plant has a name?" He knew he sounded like a moron, but he couldn't help himself.

"Well, I can't call her *hey you* when I talk to her, can I? The poor thing would get offended."

Nicholas gave up. He wasn't even going to ask. If he did, he'd end up as crazy as Emily.

He knelt down and inspected the area where the planter had stood. Cunningly blended into the pattern of the floorboards was the faint outline of a square. Fixed on one side was a metal catch, so small he had trouble grasping it with his large fingers. When he finally had enough purchase, he pulled it up, removing the fake section of flooring with it and exposing the safe hidden underneath.

"What's the combination?"

"Oh, that's easy. My birth date."

He looked at her with a stunned gaze. He had a sudden mental picture of the dossier on Emily Payne, containing, among other things, her date of birth. "You use your birthday? Anyone could crack that. That's one of the first things they'd try."

Emily shrugged. "No one knows the safe is there. Well, almost no one. Anyway, I kept forgetting the combination. At least I don't forget my own birthday."

Nicholas groaned and ran his hand through his hair in frustration.

"I don't understand why you're upset. It makes perfect sense to me."

"I'll reset the combination to a new configuration. One that can't be easily cracked. And before you ask, *I'll* remember the numbers for you. In fact, while I'm here, *I'll* be the one who puts the papyrus away, okay?"

He spun the dial in the front of the safe. First left, right, and left again. Picking up the plastic sleeve, he dropped it inside, closed the door and spun the dial again. In short order, he inserted the cover, lifted the fern, planter and all, and placed it back in its original position.

As he stood up, he patted one of the fern fronds and muttered, "There you go, Abigail. All safe and sound."

He spun and faced her, a frown on his face, silently daring her to make a comment. "We'd better have dinner before it's ruined," he mumbled and stomped out of the room, headed for the kitchen.

Behind his back, Emily had to bite the inside of her cheek to stop herself chuckling. Nicholas's somber façade had started to slip. She grinned. Emily would bet odds he'd never talked to a plant in his life. If he wasn't careful, before he knew where he was, he'd actually be laughing out loud.

No one should be that serious about life all the time. It would do him good to loosen up a bit. Shame he had to be so touchy about everything though.

"The steak will only take another few minutes," Nicholas said as she entered the kitchen. "Have a glass of wine while you wait. I found a bottle of very acceptable red hidden in the back of one of the cupboards."

"I'd forgotten it was there." Emily pulled a chair up to the table. "It was a present from one of my students last Christmas. I'm amazed you found enough food to eat, let alone a bottle of wine to go with it."

She filled one of the wine glasses and took a sip, sighing in appreciation. Nicholas really had outdone himself. The table was beautifully set with her best silver and crystal. She fingered the lace tablecloth. Good gracious, she hadn't used this in years. Normally she grabbed something to eat and headed into the living room to watch television, her plate on her lap.

Nicholas appeared quite at home in the kitchen. She watched as he bent to flip the steaks over under the broiler. Her libido edged up a notch as her gaze lovingly followed the shape of taut buttocks outlined by the tight blue denim. She lowered her eyes to hide her hunger as he turned toward the table with a hot casserole dish cradled on a tea towel.

"Mmm, scalloped potatoes. My favorite," she murmured to fill in the silence.

He placed a crystal bowl of fresh green salad on the table and expertly transferred the steaks onto white bone-china plates. After placing one before Emily, he joined her, arranging his long legs under the table. As his knee bumped her leg, she dragged in a shaky breath. Fancy being turned on by the feel of a man's leg.

"I've fed the cat and let her out into the garden. I'll bring her in before we go to bed," Nicholas said as he served himself some salad.

"Uh, Ria. Right. I was just going to ask you about her." *Oh, Emily, what a great big fib that is.* She hadn't given poor Ria a single thought. Her mind was too full of the picture of Nicholas's long legs twining with hers, holding her tight as he—

For heaven's sake, Emily, get with the program. Damn it, she had to get her mind off her, or rather, Nicholas's body. The man was gay.

But what if he isn't, if he only thinks he is?

Emily took herself firmly in hand and concentrated on her meal, enjoying it all the more because she hadn't prepared it herself. The man was a treasure. He'd make some man a good husband one day.

Quit it, Emily.

When the first course was finished, Nicholas brought out a plate of peeled and sliced peaches and set it on the table. "This was all I could find for dessert. We'll have to do something about your grocery supplies or we'll both starve."

Forget the groceries. Emily had something else in mind—the next step in her self-appointed project.

She picked up a slice of peach and made a big production of licking it all over before she ever so slowly held it part way in her mouth, swirling her tongue around it. She almost gave into a desire to burst out laughing when Nicholas gulped and focused his attention on her lips. His breathing had grown hoarse in the silent room. Perspiration broke out on his forehead. His eyes took on a glazed look and he squirmed in the seat, as if he'd suddenly become uncomfortable. Or maybe turned on?

Okay, so she was acting like a tease, but she needed to know for certain which way Nicholas swung. If she had to employ devious methods to find out what she needed to know, so be it.

Sucking the peach sliver into her mouth, she swallowed. With Nicholas's gaze firmly focused on her, she trailed the tip of her tongue along her bottom lip to catch the last of the peach juice. Nicholas groaned and lowered his head into his hands for a second.

Oh yeah, things were heating up. Now to push it a step further.

"Nicholas, can I ask you something?" She didn't wait for an answer. "Have you always been gay? Or is this something you've just decided on?"

Nicholas gagged as he tried to swallow the slice of fruit he'd just popped into his mouth. He started to cough and splutter, his face turning a weird shade of red. Emily jumped out of her chair and ran around the table to thump him on the back. When he'd finally caught his breath, she took her seat again, staring expectantly at him as she waited for an answer to her question.

"Being gay isn't something you just decide on," he croaked. "You're either gay, or you're not."

"But when did you know? Have you ever been out with a woman?"

"I'll kill Marty for this," he muttered.

Emily frowned. "What's Marty got to do with whether you're gay or not?" She shrugged, not wanting to get sidetracked. "Sooo…have you? Been out with a woman, that is."

"Yes, but—"

"Well, perhaps that's it." *Yes!* There was hope for her yet. "Maybe you're not really gay. You probably haven't been with the right woman."

She picked up another slice of fruit and ran it across her lips before holding it out to him. He leaned forward and took it into his mouth, his lips brushing her fingers at the same time. Emily had to work hard to keep her hand from trembling. Crap, she was supposed to be turning him on, not herself.

"This is not open for discussion," he said in his official, no-nonsense voice.

"Oh, lighten up, Nicholas. You don't have to be serious all the time."

Before he could answer her, there was a sharp rat-tat-tat on the front door. "Visitors." Emily jumped up from the table and whirled out of the kitchen, glad of a chance to leave him for a few minutes in order to get her rampaging hormones under control.

"Emily, wait. Don't open the door."

As she made her way down the hallway, a crash sounded from the kitchen, as if Nicholas had knocked over the chair in his haste to get up. He hopped his way up the hallway after her, trying to pull his weapon out of the ankle holster at the same time.

"Dammit, you should have stayed in the kitchen," he whispered. "You don't know who's out there." He moved in front of her and reached out to unlock the door, his gun hidden behind his back.

"That's why I waited for you to open it," she quipped. "I'm not a total flake all the time." She knew they had to be careful, but a burglar wasn't going to waltz right up to the door and knock for admittance.

She peered around Nicholas's shoulder as he pulled the door open. Her eyes opened wide when she saw who their visitor was.

"Maxwell. What are you doing here?" Emily stared at him, her face devoid of any welcoming warmth.

"I came to see if you're okay and to let you know how your lectures went. Aren't you going to invite me in?"

She wanted to slam the door in his face. "Of course. Please come in."

As he leaned down to kiss her, she turned her head, ignoring the flash of anger on his face when his kiss landed on her cheek. A surge of annoyance rushed through her when he sauntered in and headed for the living room where he sprawled on her little couch. *Nothing like making yourself at home.*

For the first few minutes, he fussed with the crease of his trousers, unbuttoned his suit jacket and smoothed his hand down over the lapels, checking for wrinkles.

He hadn't changed. He was still more conscious of his own image than anything else going on around him. She couldn't resist having a dig at him. "Is that a new suit, Maxwell? Coming up in the world, I see. I wouldn't have thought you could afford something like that."

"Oh, I do all right, Em, old girl. And how about you? Why don't you come sit down and tell me all about it?"

Emily couldn't think of any reason for ignoring his request. She perched gingerly on the couch beside him, closing her eyes briefly when his arm immediately descended on her shoulder.

What the hell was going on here? She and Maxwell had hardly spoken to each other for the last twelve months, and suddenly he was all concerned about how she was doing? Bullshit.

Nicholas left his position at the entrance to the living room and strolled casually over to a vacant chair. Emily jumped to her feet and moved to stand beside him. "Maxwell, have you met Nicholas, my—"

"Nicholas Farley, Emily's very good friend," Nicholas interrupted before she could finish the sentence.

Maxwell pushed himself lazily to his feet and approached Nicholas. "Maxwell D'Lacey, at your service. A *very* old friend of Emily's. We go way back." He extended his hand to Nicholas at the same time as he placed his other arm about Emily's waist.

"I thought you were just another lecturer from the university?"

"Oh, I'm much more than that, aren't I, Em?" He pulled her close, dropping a light kiss on her cheek.

Emily tried to edge away, but he had too tight a hold on her. "*Actually*, Maxwell, we're nothing more than work colleagues." She pried his fingers from her waist and stepped away from him.

"Ahh, but we were once much more." He chuckled. "Hey, we had a lot of fun, Em, and could have again if you'll only say the word."

What the effing hell? Maxwell knew there would never again be anything between them, so why act like this? It was almost as if he were trying to make Nicholas jealous.

He prowled around the room, running his fingers over the furniture, touching her belongings as if assessing their worth. Emily wanted to smack him one.

"So how's the translating going, Em, old girl? All done?"

She burst out laughing. "You're kidding, right? You know how hard it is to translate that stuff. It'll be a few more days yet."

Maxwell moved closer and slid his finger down the curve of her cheek. "How about you let me see? Where is it? Safely hidden away? I might be able to help you with the translation."

In a pig's eye. Maxwell was a poor lecturer at best, and a lousy historian. He'd be no help at all. He just wanted to ride on her coat tails again, gaining kudos in the academic field on her knowledge. No way would she let him see the papyrus. Before she could tell him that, Nicholas intervened.

"That's right, the papyrus is locked up at the moment. I'm looking after it...and Emily."

"You? But I thought you were nothing but a friend. How come—"

"Aah, I'm more than just a friend, I'm living with Emily." He rested his arm about her shoulders.

Nicholas had to control his grin when the other man's eyes opened wide at this statement. Anger flashed across Maxwell's face and it was all Nicholas could do not to crow. He knew he was being juvenile, but he couldn't help himself. Maxwell D'Lacey grated on him, more so when he tried to lay claim to Emily.

It was more than mild annoyance at the man's presumption. It was anger, plain and simple. It surged through his blood, making him want to reach out and grab this stuffed-shirt, pompous twit and shake him by his perfectly pressed lapels.

It came to him in a flash. He was jealous of any other man touching Emily. His mouth fell open in shock. Him? Jealous?

That had never happened before. Love-‘em-and-leave-‘em Farley. That was him.

He pushed the thought to the back of his mind to deal with later. Right now, he had to get rid of this bozo before he knocked his perfect teeth down his throat.

Releasing his hold on Emily, he grasped Maxwell by the arm and started to move him toward the door. “Emily and I were just finishing up dinner when you interrupted. I’m sure you’ll excuse us.”

Maxwell didn’t have time to respond. Nicholas had him outside the front door almost before he could draw breath.

“Thanks for calling in to see how *old Em* is, but don’t worry. I’ll be looking after her from now on.” He slammed the door and turned to face Emily, mentally dusting off his hands.

“Nicholas, that was a bit rude.”

“Rude, nothing. The man is a sleaze. While we’re on the subject, how come you didn’t tell me about him?”

“What’s to tell? He’s just another lecturer at the university.”

“You two obviously have history. And the man would like a bit more of the same, thank you very much.”

Nicholas felt the anger rise to the surface, heard it color his voice, making it strident and harsh. He knew the anger wasn’t just because Emily hadn’t told him about Maxwell. It was more, much more, than that. It was jealousy. Possessiveness. And a deadly need to thrash anyone who came within spitting distance of Emily.

Yep, he was jealous. With a capital J. And if he wasn’t careful, Emily would know it too.

“Don’t get bent out of shape, Nicholas.”

Her voice was so calm it fueled his anger even more. He fought to rein it in before it spilled over into a blazing row. *This is a job, Nicholas. Remember that.*

"So what's with you and what's-his-name?" he demanded.

"Maxwell and I had a long-term relationship. It ended about twelve months ago. Now we're colleagues. Nothing else. The only reason he came around now is he wants some of the glory of translating the papyrus. He trades on other people's successes."

"Is that why you broke up?"

"No, I found I didn't love him and I couldn't stand living with him." She wandered back into the kitchen, Nicholas following her. "He was more concerned with his own good looks than our relationship. He's also a gambler and a womanizer. He'd tell me he was working late and I'd find out he was at the casino with another woman. *And* it was my money he was gambling with."

"I get the feeling there's a lot more to it than that. I could sense the vibes coming off you back there in the living room. Maxwell D'Lacey sure thinks he can still lay claim to you."

She started to clear the table, stacking the dishes on the sink. "Okay, so it wasn't that simple. I'm not about to go into the tale of Maxwell's dirty little deceptions. Suffice it to say if there's one thing I can't stand, it's finding out someone has lied to me and made a fool of me. As far as I'm concerned, there's no excuse that would make that acceptable."

Nicholas clenched his fists as Emily turned on the tap and started to rinse off the dishes. He had a sinking feeling in the pit of his stomach. After that statement, how could he tell her he wasn't gay? She'd never forgive him for lying to her. Marty may have made up the story as a means of getting him into her house, but he'd gone along with it.

He suddenly found he *did* want to tell her, but he knew he couldn't. She hadn't finished translating the papyrus and the assignment came first. Damn Marty for putting him in this situation. When she found out he wasn't gay, she'd throw him out on his ass. He had a choice. Tell her now and risk the assignment, or wait and try to break it to her gently later. Neither option appealed, but he decided to wait.

It wasn't only because of the papyrus. He wanted these few days with Emily, even if he had to continue the pretense. Hell, he'd only known her one day and already she'd sneaked under his normal defenses. One thing was for certain, she sure did something for his libido. The blood pounded through his veins every time he thought about the scene in the kitchen.

For once, he wanted to break his self-imposed rule of no long-term relationships while he was an agent for the federal government. He had a strange feeling Emily could turn out to be more than just a body to protect. He couldn't believe how many times he'd had to remind himself this was nothing but a job. And thinking of jobs...

"One other thing, Emily. Don't rush to the door if anyone knocks again."

"Hey, I told you I wasn't going to open it until you got there."

"Doesn't matter. You put yourself in danger by not waiting for me. Next time, you stay behind me, out of the way. Is that clear?"

"But it was only Maxwell."

"This time. Just wait for me in future. And if Maxwell D'Lacey turns up again, I'll deal with him." *Gladly*, he thought as a number of grim scenarios flitted through his mind.

"Forget Maxwell. All that's in the past. Why don't you watch television while I clear the kitchen? You cooked, I'll clean."

Emily's voice cut across the thoughts whizzing around in his brain, threatening to drive him crazy. "Right. I'll do that. But first I'll ring Marty and get him to drop some groceries over tomorrow."

"There's a phone in the hallway and another extension in the bedroom. Take your pick."

"Anything special you want? In the grocery line, I mean."

"Not particularly. I eat most things."

Nicholas was glad to vacate the kitchen. He needed some time on his own to sort out his feelings. He couldn't believe he'd felt jealous of that twerp, Maxwell. He hadn't cared enough in the past to have violent feelings for any of the women he'd dated. Yet here he was with a bad case of the jealousies over a woman he'd just met.

How the hell had that happened?

He was a sane, sensible man. A man who lived by rules rather than his emotions. He was reacting like a schoolboy. His cock was hard enough to do him an injury, his gut twisted into knots because of a relationship in Emily's past. What the fuck was going on here?

He didn't believe in love at first sight. That was a phrase coined for women and romance books. It didn't happen in real life.

Or did it?

Chapter Four

Emily stacked the last of the plates in the dishwasher and turned the machine on. Drying off the wine glasses they'd used, she stored them safely away. A final wipe of the bench and she was finished. She was all set to join Nicholas.

She found herself hesitating. There was so much going on inside her mind she couldn't think straight. Something wasn't right with this whole situation, but damned if she could work out what it was. Had she missed something? Something vitally important and not just to the project at hand? Why did she have the feeling it was of the utmost importance to her personally to find out what it was?

Another thing... She'd reacted to Nicholas like she'd never reacted to any man before. Not even Maxwell. Her bodyguard only had to look at her for her blood to heat up and her heart to start racing, but it was more than just a physical thing. He touched something deep inside of her. Made her think of the impossible.

And it *was* impossible. Because Nicholas was gay.

Or was he?

She was positive he'd responded to her as a woman. His body language gave him away. A momentary grin flashed across her face as she remembered the intriguing bulge outlined by his tight denims.

The grin disappeared as she continued to worry at the problem. Something was definitely happening between her and the sexy bodyguard. The tension between them when they were eating dinner had been so thick, it's a wonder they hadn't choked on it.

So was he or wasn't he? And if not, what should she do about it?

Before she came up with a satisfactory answer to the questions swimming in her brain, a loud thump sounded on the front door.

"Dammit, don't tell me Maxwell has returned." Emily silently cursed as she hung up the dishcloth. "Doesn't that man know the meaning of the word *no*?"

Mindful of Nicholas's rules, she hovered at the entrance to the kitchen until Nicholas was in place behind the front door, his weapon held at the ready. With a quick glance at her, he opened the door a crack and peered out.

"Yeah? Can I help you?"

"Oh...I came to see Emily. I wasn't expecting anyone else to be here. Is she in?" a sultry feminine voice asked.

Emily pushed past Nicholas, recognizing the voice immediately. "Miranda? What are you doing here?"

"Emily. It's been ages since I've heard from you and even longer since I've seen you." She shrugged. "I decided to correct the oversight."

Emily narrowed her eyes as Nicholas eyeballed the woman who stepped over the threshold. Would he react to her as every other red-blooded male within spitting distance normally did?

Miranda wasn't as tall as Emily, but she had a luscious body, curved in all the right places. She wore her clothes like a model, her outfits designed to make the most of her figure. All in all, she was a sexy package and she always got her man.

"Nicholas, this is Miranda Davenport, an old friend."

"Less of the old," Miranda retorted lightly. "I'm six months younger than you."

Nicholas, the gun hidden behind his back, extended his hand to shake Miranda's. When he quickly released the proffered hand and stepped back, Emily felt unaccountably pleased. She didn't want her friend to collect this particular scalp. Emily was suddenly relieved Nicholas was gay and immune to Miranda's brand of allure.

Hang on a minute, how silly can a person get? If he *were* gay, Miranda couldn't have him either.

"Want me to disappear so you two can have some privacy?"

"No, it's okay. You finish watching your show. We'll go upstairs. That way, we won't disturb you."

She hustled Miranda upstairs and into the bedroom, flopping onto the bed while Miranda took up her favorite position in the rocking chair, her legs slung over the side.

"You sly dog, Emily. How come you've got that gorgeous hunk living here with you? The last I heard, you were off men, particularly handsome ones."

Emily turned over onto her stomach and propped her chin in her hands. "It's all to do with that papyrus I found. It's a long story, but basically, the government wants it after I've translated it, but so does someone else. My office at the university was broken into and trashed."

"But what about the hunk?" Miranda interrupted. "Where does he fit in?"

"He's my bodyguard."

Miranda raised her eyebrows. "Your what?"

"My bodyguard." Emily couldn't help the cheesy grin that slid across her face.

"Hey, lucky you."

"And he's gay."

Miranda burst out laughing. "Oh, poor Emily. All that man and you can't even hit on him."

"Stop with the smart cracks, old friend. That's the problem. He says he's gay. Or rather, Agent Tomlins said he was and Nicholas hasn't denied it. But I'm not certain he is. Maybe he just thinks he is."

All sign of merriment wiped from her face, Miranda sat up straight in the rocking chair. "Okay, all jokes aside. What makes you think he's not gay?"

"He reacts to me like any normal man. Forget the fact he pushes all *my* buttons. There's just something about him. He watches me when I'm eating. And I swear I heard him groan when I licked the peach juice off my lips, even though he tried to cover it with a cough. I know he was turned on. If he wanted to hide the fact, he shouldn't wear tight jeans."

"Ah ha, the plot thickens. Tell me more."

"What if he's not really gay? Maybe he hasn't met the right woman yet?"

"And you want to be that woman?" Miranda vacated the rocking chair and paced about the room. "Well, there *is* one way to find out. Vamp the man. See if he responds to your overtures."

"How the hell do I do that? I'm not sophisticated like you."

"This isn't about sophistication. This is about sex." She strode over to the chest of drawers and pulled out a handful of frothy underwear. "Emily, for all you don't care about fashion, you have the sexiest underwear of anyone I know. Try strutting your stuff in one of these next-to-nothing scraps of lace and see what response you get."

"Come to think of it, he did react strangely when I stripped in front of him earlier."

Miranda spun about to face Emily, her eyes wide in surprise. "You what? You stripped down in front of him?" A gurgle of laughter escaped her. "I don't believe it."

"Well, I did make him turn his back *and* I thought he was gay," Emily excused herself. "And I didn't take *all* my clothes off. Besides, it shouldn't have bothered him at all. That's my point. I think the idea of it did bother him." She paused a moment in thought before going on. "Could it be as simple as that, do you think? Try and vamp the man and see what comes up?"

She started to chuckle as she realized how she'd phrased it. "If *that* comes up, I'll know I'm on the right track. If the boner I saw in his jeans is any indication, the man is huge. No way would I miss that."

"Been checking the goods out, have we?" Miranda chortled. "Anyway, give it a shot. You won't know unless you try. Up the sexual tension. Flaunt yourself. Grab any opportunity you're presented with to get close to him. Touch him. Hell, manufacture the opportunities if necessary. You'll soon find out if he's confused about his sexuality." She paused a moment. "Or...maybe he's lying and isn't really gay at all. Have you thought of that?"

Emily sat upright on the bed. "No, I can't believe he'd lie about something like this. A man's not going to say he's gay if he isn't. Hetero men get bent out of shape about things like that. Anyway, I told him how I feel about people lying to me." She swung her legs over the side of the bed and pushed herself to her feet. "No, I just think maybe the poor man is mixed up."

"Then initiate him into the pleasures of a relationship with a woman. Seduce him. A word of warning, though. Find out first if he's been practicing safe sex. *And* how many relationships he has been involved in."

Miranda walked over to the rocking chair and picked up her purse. "Now, I have to go. This was just a flying visit. I'm meeting James for a late dinner." She opened her purse, pulled out a handful of foil-wrapped packages and tossed them into the bowl beside the bed. "I've bought you some new ones to add to the collection. These are glow in the dark. Extra Large."

"You're going to have to stop wasting your money on these things. They'll never get used."

"Why not?" Miranda grinned. "You've got the perfect candidate right here in the house with you. Get the sexy bodyguard to try out the new ones for size. You'll be able to see him coming *and* going in the dark."

A gurgle of laughter escaped Emily as she followed her friend out of the bedroom.

Miranda paused on the first step and looked back over her shoulder at Emily. "There's one other thing. Don't get your hopes up too high. *You* might think the man is just confused about his sexuality, but he really could be gay. I don't want you hurt."

"It'll be okay. If he doesn't react to me walking around in nothing but my sheer silk teddy, I'll give it a miss. The shop guaranteed it would turn on even the most cold-blooded male."

"You mean the pale pink one? The one that actually looks as if you have nothing on at all? Well, if that doesn't work, nothing will." She moved down the staircase, her high heels clicking on the polished wood.

"Bye, Nicholas. Hope to see you again." She halted at the entrance and whispered in an aside to Emily, "Give me a ring and let me know how it goes."

Emily closed and locked the door after her, resting back against it. Could she do this? She'd never vamped a man in her life. But she was good at carrying out projects. This would be just another project.

Project: Man—how to initiate Nicholas into the joys of loving a woman.

ꟿ

Nicholas knew the moment Emily stepped foot inside the living room. He would have been conscious of her presence even if he'd been deaf. When she placed a tray of coffee on the low table in front of the couch and dropped down beside him, he released a pent-up breath. At least he knew where she was now, knew she was safe beside him. After all, that was his assignment, keeping Emily safe.

What a load of crap, a little voice echoed inside his mind. *This has nothing to do with your assignment.*

He was honest enough with himself to acknowledge the truth of the statement. This had more to do with Emily herself. He had committed the unpardonable sin of getting emotionally involved with his case. With Emily. All in one afternoon. How the fuck had that happened?

"Good show?"

"Hmm, it's a documentary about opening up one of the tombs in the Valley of the Kings in Egypt. Very involving." He didn't tell her he'd hardly taken in a word as he'd waited for her to join him. He'd found himself straining to catch the faint echoes of her voice drifting down from the upper floor. Her friend had seemed nice, but, dammit, he'd wanted Emily here with him.

Now she was and he couldn't concentrate on the show at all.

"That's the dig my friend is on." Emily curled her feet under her and rested her shoulder against Nicholas.

"Huh?" Shit, he'd lost track of the conversation, his mind totally taken up with the feeling of Emily's warmth reaching out to him. He felt like an idiot.

She pointed to the television screen. "The friend who sent me the pot with the papyrus in it. The Egyptian government invited him to join that dig. If we watch carefully, we might even see him."

Nicholas didn't give a shit for anyone on the show. Hell, he didn't even know what the guy looked like. Nor did he care. He was more interested in Emily. If he lifted his arm a bit—just...like...that—he could settle it around her shoulders.

He'd heard women say gay men made the best of friends. Maybe Emily would see the move as nothing more than one friend hugging another. He felt like a raw schoolboy, sitting in the movies with his first girlfriend, pretending to stretch as a means of getting his arm around his girl.

He waited for Emily's reaction. When she only snuggled closer, he tightened his hold until her head rested on his shoulder. They sat like that for a few minutes before Emily leaned forward and picked up the two coffee cups, handing one to Nicholas.

"I hope you take milk and sugar. I never thought to ask before I made it."

"Yeah, that's fine." No way would he tell her he hated his coffee with sugar. She'd immediately want to make him a fresh cup and he liked her just where she was, snuggled down beside him. Not for anything would he break up this moment voluntarily.

He sipped at his drink, breathing in the aroma of freshly brewed coffee. Another perfume tantalized his senses. He leaned closer to Emily and breathed deeply, his eyes closed. It was the scent of shampoo, or some type of body lotion. *Flowers.* She smelled like flowers, as if she'd rolled in the mass of color in her back garden.

Emily grinned from behind her coffee mug. Well, she'd made a good start on her project. She wouldn't have believed it'd be so easy to get Nicholas to put his arm around her. She slid a fraction closer, pressing against his side, her head once again on his shoulder.

The coffee cup held in one hand, she casually lowered her other hand until it rested on his thigh. *Let's see how he reacts to this.*

The muscles under her hand flexed. She felt the tension grip his body. Heard him draw in a sharp breath. Suddenly, it ceased to be a game. Or if it was, she was caught up in it too.

She tried to concentrate on what was happening on the television, but to no avail. She was too conscious of Nicholas. His heat reached out to her, firing her senses, filling her with an immediate rush of hormones at his nearness. God help her, she wanted him. Bad.

As she slowly slid her hand upward, kneading the muscles of his inner thigh, his breathing grew erratic. He jerked in reaction, dragging in another deep breath, and it was all Emily could do to stop from laughing.

He'd just taken a sip of his coffee when she launched the next phase of her project. "Nicholas, have you always practiced safe sex?"

Terrific, Emily, she silently berated herself. *About as subtle as a sledgehammer.*

As he spluttered on a mouthful of the hot liquid and started to choke, Emily quickly put her cup down and twisted around to face him. She pulled herself up onto her knees and thumped him on the back. This was *not* the response she was hoping for.

It seemed to take a long time, but finally Nicholas had his coughing under control and was able to breathe again. Well, sort of. The sound rattled in his chest, causing guilt to flood through Emily. Damn, she didn't want to kill the man. Just make him notice her.

"It's okay now," he gasped, his voice hoarse and deep. "The coffee. It went down the wrong way."

Emily took the cup from him and placed it on the table beside her own. "Are you sure you're okay?"

She watched as he breathed deeply, only the occasional cough interrupting the flow of oxygen to his lungs. Taking a handkerchief from his pocket, he wiped his watery eyes.

"Yeah, I'm fine now. Sorry about that." He leaned forward, picked up his cup and took a swift gulp. There was silence as he finished off the coffee.

"So do you?"

"Do I what?"

"Do you, or rather, have you always practiced safe sex? I mean, we hear all the statistics on TV, particularly in reference to gay men."

Nicholas gulped. *Bloody hell, she's like a dog with a bone.* He could see she wasn't about to give up. He'd have to answer her. "Yes, I've always been very careful. No, I am not one of those statistics. I have no dreaded diseases and to my knowledge there are no children out there looking for their daddy."

Emily pounced on his last words. "Ah ha, so the relationships you've had with women have been physical." She sat back with a pleased smile on her face.

"Marty, you're dead meat," he muttered.

"I'm sorry, I didn't quite hear that."

"It's nothing." Nicholas jumped up from the couch, putting distance between them before he was tempted to grab her and kiss her senseless. Before he was stupid enough to tell her they had all lied to her. And, damn it, he wanted to. He wanted to end this farce. How the fuck was he supposed to go on acting as if he were gay when he wanted her so badly?

"I'm going to have a shower." He backed away from the couch. "It's time for bed anyway. It's been a long day."

"Don't forget to bring the cat in before you go up."

"No problem. I'll do that now." He left the room as if his worst nightmares were coming after him.

Emily grinned and hugged herself. *Well, there you go*, she thought, pleased with her discovery. The man may not be gay after all. He just needed a good woman to love him. Was it possible she was that woman? She had a strange feeling this moment was important to her future.

She heard him call for Ria and lock the back door. Smiling as the third tread from the top creaked loudly, giving away his position, she tracked his movements up the staircase. When the bathroom door closed, she yawned.

Nicholas was right. It was time for bed. She had a sudden mental image of the two of them lying in her four-poster bed, snuggled together. Nicholas would gather her close, his hand sliding—

"Stop it, Emily. One step at a time. Don't rush this. And anyway, he's not sleeping with you, he's sleeping on the damn floor."

She pushed the erotic images from her head and quickly tidied the room, fluffing the cushions on the couch. Gathering up her purse and glasses, she looked around for her house keys. When a further search proved fruitless, she shrugged and pushed the matter from her mind. They'd turn up in time.

Picking up the tray with the empty coffee cups, she deposited it in the kitchen before she made her way upstairs, clicking off lights as she went. The bathroom door squeaked at the same moment the third tread from the top groaned in protest at her weight. She paused and looked up, her momentum suddenly halted. Even if a herd of elephants had been chasing her, she wouldn't have been able to move.

Nicholas stood in the open doorway, backlit by the soft glow of the bathroom light. He was perfectly naked but for a pair of black satin boxers. And *perfect* was the right word. Nicholas in tight jeans and tee shirt was disturbing. Nicholas in the flesh, so to speak, was just...well, mind-blowing was the only word she could think of for the moment.

"Wow," she whispered. Her brain had totally shut down.

There wasn't an ounce of spare flesh anywhere. Everything was muscle, well toned, perfectly delineated. A smattering of dark hair spread across his sculptured chest and arrowed downward, until it disappeared beneath the band of the boxers riding low on his hips.

Emily had a burning need to run her hands across his chest, feel the warmth of his skin, follow the line of dark hair down over his flat stomach. She wanted to slide her mouth along—

"Is there a problem, Emily?"

She swallowed. "Ah...I, ah, I was just wondering where Ria was," she finished in a rush.

"She raced up the stairs ahead of me when I let her in."

"She's probably in the bedroom. She normally sleeps on the end of my bed. Although she's always loved that airbed so don't be surprised if she takes up residence there."

"Not with me on it, she doesn't," he retorted.

Emily didn't reply. Instead, she stared, her mouth dry with longing, as Nicholas walked into the bedroom. The back view was as impressive as the front. The cutest set of buns she'd seen in a long time. She tightened her grip on the timber balustrade until the joints in her fingers protested. The pain broke the sensual haze obliterating her normal rational thinking.

Get a grip, Emily. God, she was an idiot at times. She'd let a perfectly good opportunity pass her by. This was supposed to be a work-in-progress and she'd stood there like a love-struck teenager. *Use your intelligence, girl, don't let your hormones take over.*

She snorted. *Impossible.* Impossible or not, she'd just have to work with what she had. She needed to get this project underway. All that logical thinking disappeared when she heard Nicholas's voice from the bedroom.

"Come to bed, Emily."

Nicholas had obviously found her linen cupboard. The blow-up mattress was made up with crisp white sheets and one of the spare quilts, not that he'd need the extra covering in the summer heat.

Ignoring the enticing sight of Nicholas laying with his arms clasped over his head, Emily walked straight over to the chest of drawers, dumping her purse and glasses on the top. Sliding out the first drawer, she searched for a nightgown amid the jumble of soft laces and slinky satins. A swatch of sheer fabric caught her attention. She slid her hand under it to lift it up. Could she do it? Did she dare?

She didn't need her glasses to know this was the pale pink teddy—it was the only totally sheer one she owned—but perhaps the see-through fabric was a little *too* blatant this early in the project. She studied it for a moment before discarding it. She didn't want to scare the poor guy off all together—just whet his appetite.

Pushing the blaze of colors to one side, she reached for the packet lying on the bottom of the drawer. This one she hadn't even opened yet. Maybe now was a good time to christen it and most men seemed to like black lace. At least, that's what all the women's magazines said. *Let's see if it has any effect on Nicholas.*

"I'm going to have a shower. Won't be long," she said as she scuttled out of the room.

Nicholas watched her leave, the sheet pulled up to his waist. He already knew what she wore under her clothes. Now to see what she wore to bed.

He groaned, the sound long and pitiful, as he heard the shower go on. His mind immediately supplied a lurid picture of Emily, naked, the warm water cascading over her body, making her skin slick and—

"Aw, hell, stop it, Nicholas. You'll never get through the night if you keep this up."

It was all very well and good giving himself a stern talking to. Shame it didn't work. The bowl of condoms on the bedside table seemed to beckon him. He couldn't help but fantasize about what he'd like to do with each and every one.

He heard the shower turn off and waited. When Emily appeared in the doorway, he felt as if he'd been punched in the gut. The air left his chest in a rush and he was almost light-headed as he gazed at her.

Holy fuck. He'd always had a thing for black lace. Forget the invisible paint, Emily in this black lace concoction could be the army's next secret weapon. Every soldier, both allied and enemy alike, would lay down his weapon and grovel at her feet.

He groaned softly as he eyed the tiny lace cups molding her breasts so lovingly. His gaze slid down, following the line of her body. The black fabric ended abruptly just above her hip, the teddy cut so high at the sides, it made it seem like her legs went on for ever.

Pale skin shone through the open weave of the lace, taking on a luminescence almost ethereal in its beauty. Her dark hair hung down to her shoulders and her beautiful topaz eyes glowed. A Mona Lisa smile flitted across her face as she watched him watching her.

Oh boy, his every fantasy come true. Then he remembered he had to sleep in the same room as this vision. *Ah, crap!*

His mouth dried, his brain turned to mush. He couldn't formulate even one intelligent thought. Talk about an army. He felt like a wild hoard of testosterone-filled warriors had invaded his bloodstream, all marching rapidly downward toward that one part of his anatomy he desperately needed to keep under control.

He wiped his hand over his face, just to check his tongue wasn't hanging out, his gaze never leaving the enticing goddess posing in the bedroom doorway. Emily turned sideway and leaned back against the doorframe, her body arched, her face turned toward him.

She slid her hand up so it rested on the timber above her. Then she bent one long, tapering leg until her foot balanced against the doorframe as well. Now she looked like a pin-up girl on an old wartime calendar. She arched her body even further, her breasts in danger of escaping the constriction of the fragile black lace. She pouted her lips and fluttered her eyelashes at him.

Lord help him, she really *was* posing for him. His lips twitched as he fought to control the sudden laughter building up inside him. Not that he didn't appreciate the sight. She was as sexy as hell and his body was busy reinforcing what his brain had already cottoned on to. He wanted this woman more than any woman he'd ever been involved with.

No, it was the look on her face that made him want to laugh. She'd contorted her features into what she obviously considered a sexy, come-hither expression. She'd knock herself out if she kept batting her eyelashes like that. The pout made her look more like she'd just sucked on a lemon, and if she moved her supporting leg another inch, she'd fall flat on her delectable derrière.

Even as the thought filtered into his brain, she started to slide, arms flailing as she sought to retain her balance. Nicholas had a hard time stopping himself laughing outright. He didn't want to offend her.

Emily started to chuckle. He liked a woman who could laugh at herself.

"So much for that. A femme fatale I'm not."

Hands on her hips, chest thrust out, head held high, she strutted across the room. Her hips swayed in exaggerated motion, like a model on a catwalk. When she rounded the end of the bed, she spoiled the whole performance by stubbing her toe. He worked hard to control the twitching of his lips and held his breath, sure he was going to lose it. Suddenly she tripped, slipped down and disappeared below the level of the mattress.

Nicholas couldn't help himself. He finally let go, his laughter filling the bedroom. He reached over to lift the cover and peered under the bed. Emily was on her hands and knees, tangled in the lace overhang of the bedcover.

She looked at him through a curtain of dark hair, a grin on her face. "It's okay. I just thought it was a perfect time to check for dust bunnies under the bed. Can't be too careful, you know. They're wily little things at the best of times."

She poked her head right under the bed as if really looking for some sly, elusive creature.

Nicholas was still chuckling as he climbed out of his makeshift bed to help Emily to her feet. "Come on out of there. The dust bunnies will still be alive and kicking tomorrow."

The laughter died in his throat as he took in the picture of black lace and soft white bedcover, and even paler skin shining through. His mouth went dry and his heart began to race as the image imprinted itself on his brain, a study in contrasts.

Emily didn't need to act the femme fatale. She didn't have to try hard to be sexy. She just was, without any effort at all.

Once Emily was upright again, Nicholas dropped her hand and scooted back around the end of the bed to his mattress. If he didn't put some distance between them, he'd end up begging her to take him in with her.

He threw himself down, turned his back to Emily and pulled the sheet up to his shoulder. With a heartfelt prayer that sleep would come quickly, he closed his eyes.

Didn't make any difference. He may not be able to see, but his ears weren't painted on. He heard the springs squeak as Emily climbed into bed. Registered the click as she turned off the bedside lamp and plunged the room into darkness. A few more squeaks as she settled herself and then silence. Maybe now he'd actually be able to fall asleep. Then he heard something else. A hissing sound. Was that Ria? He lifted his head from the pillow and listened.

He bit back a groan as he realized what it was. The airbed had sprung a leak. And given the way it was deflating underneath him, he'd be down on the floor in no time flat. With a frustrated sigh, he climbed out of bed, found the valve and puffed a few more blasts of air into it.

Once back on the mattress, he tried to settle, turning first one way and then the other. Nothing seemed to work. He was too keyed up to sleep. And the mattress, underinflated to start with, was getting thinner and thinner. He stood it as long as he could, before he gave a loud sigh and crawled out again to replenish the air.

"Nicholas, what *are* you doing? All this tossing and turning and the agonized sighs are keeping me from getting to sleep."

"The bloody mattress has a leak. My spine keeps hitting the floor."

"Oh, for crying out loud, get up off the floor and get into bed. Otherwise neither of us will get any sleep."

The bedsprings squeaked as she moved over. Tension gripped him. His body tightened with anticipation, an anticipation that couldn't be realized. Damn, he wanted to join her oh so bad, but he knew it was a rotten idea. "Ah, no, it's okay. I don't want to deprive you of half your bed. I'm a big boy. I need lots of space."

"Don't be such an idiot. The bed is plenty big enough for the two of us. And if you're worried about sleeping with a woman, I'll put the spare pillows down the center of the bed as a barrier." She gave a loud snort. "For Christ's sake, I don't bite."

He gave up, crawled off the mattress and grabbed the weapon he'd hidden under his pillow. After transferring it surreptitiously to Emily's bed, he slipped in beside her. Her leg brushed against his as she squirmed around, repositioning the pillows.

How the hell was he supposed to sleep beside this package of pure dynamite? One more brush of that silken leg and he'd blow his cover. In more ways than one. She'd be left without any doubts at all as to whether or not he was gay.

Chapter Five

The nightmare pulled Emily into a dark abyss. Half-seen nebulous shadows projected a sense of menace as they chased her through a labyrinth of never-ending corridors. Her heart thundered in her chest. Gasping in fright, she struggled to stay one step ahead. Hands reached for her, ripping at her clothes. Sucking her down. She fought to remain conscious as a weight descended on her chest. One raspy breath drawn in. Released. Only to fight for the next.

Pain.

In her hands, her arms. Like sharp knives cutting into the flesh. A scream built up inside her, filling her mind, struggling for release. She knew it was no use—there was no one to hear her—but some indomitable part of her spirit wouldn't allow her to lie there and wait for fate to consume her, for her life to be changed forever.

Dragging in an agonized breath, she held it, the scream gathering force inside her brain. She opened her mouth to vent her rage at her helplessness, her lips pulled back in a grimace of pain...

Meow.

Emily struggled up through the layers of darkness, her subconscious mind telling her to wake up. Her heart pounded out a staccato beat, the blood racing through her veins, fed by the charge of adrenaline. Her brain felt sluggish, as if still caught in the terror of the dream. An unseen weight continued to press her down.

Meow.

She forced open leaden eyelids to see two bright yellow orbs glaring at her. It was almost enough to send her back into the nightmare. Reality took over and she focused on the cat on her chest. In her sleep, Emily had crossed her hands on her breasts in a defensive gesture and the darn cat had a firm hold, claws digging into the sensitive flesh.

"Damn it, Ria, don't do that." As she pushed herself up onto her elbows, the animal slithered down to her lap. "You scared me senseless."

Now she knew her mistress was awake, the cat bounded off the bed and raced over to the bedroom door. She turned and glared at Emily, her tail raised high in a perfect question mark. When Emily did nothing but stare at it, she stalked back and jumped up on the bed, protesting loudly, her cries becoming more distressed by the minute.

"You want to go out, I guess. Not my job. Nicholas locked the stupid cat flap. He can get up and take you out."

Emily lifted Ria, leaned over the pillow barrier, and placed her on Nicholas's chest. Her lips twitched as the cat pushed her wet nose right into his face. Ria let rip, the cry long and plaintive. *Meooww, meooww.*

To help things along, Emily poked Nicholas in the ribs.

"Wha...what's the matter?" Nicholas came awake with a start, taking an instant to orient himself.

"Ria needs to go."

He shook his head, still groggy, his normal finely tuned instincts failing him for once. "Go where?"

For the life of him, he couldn't work out what was going on. He peered down to see Emily's cat sitting on his chest, growling at him. Did cats growl? This one did—he turned his head to look at the digital display on the bedside clock—at five in the morning, dammit.

"Ria needs to go. You'll have to take her outside."

"Can't she wait?" he snarled, only to have his question answered when Ria growled again and dug sharp little claws into his bare chest. "Ouch. Okay already, cat. I'm coming."

He grabbed the beast with one arm and swung his legs over the side of the bed. Ria jumped from his arms and sprinted for the door, leaving a bloody scratch on his chest as a souvenir of her urgency. He rubbed at his abused flesh as he followed the persistent feline down the stairs and into the kitchen.

When the stubborn lock resisted his efforts, he cursed softly. With one final yank, the door opened, flying back to bang him on the knee. As he clung to the open door to take his weight off his protesting knee, Ria took off into the back garden, not at all concerned for his plight.

"Two minutes, cat. That's all you've got. Two bloody minutes."

The sensor light immediately clicked on, spotlighting the colorful scene. Favoring his bruised knee, Nicholas stepped through the doorway and took the opportunity to glance around the garden. Everything was as it should be. He would have known if anyone had activated the security light during the night. Not only would the glare have illuminated the bedroom and woken him, he'd spent a long time lying there unable to sleep last night.

His body was in a perpetual state of semi-arousal. Not exactly conducive to deep, relaxing sleep, particularly when the cause of all the upheaval lay beside him, albeit on the other side of a mound of pillows. At least she'd kept to her own side of the bed.

"Ria, your two minutes are up. Get your feline butt back inside right now."

He hadn't really expected the cat to take any notice of him. She seemed to do pretty much as she pleased. He could trace her movements through the garden simply by watching the flower heads bobbing. All he could see of the cat was the tip of her tail as she held it high.

"Okay, Ria, have it your way. I'm going back to bed for a few hours. You can stay out here and play with the flowers. And I hope they give you hayfever."

He turned to enter the house, his hand extended toward the door, and stopped dead. It suddenly felt as if the blood had frozen in his veins.

All his warrior instincts came to the fore, sharpening his sight, enhancing his hearing. He dropped to one knee and cast a swift glance over the garden again. The only movement was the waving of the flower stalks caused by the passage of the cat.

He moved closer to the door to inspect the scratches around the lock. They stood out in stark relief on the stained timber, like fresh-cut wounds on a pristine surface. Somebody had tried to get into the house. He'd been awake until three at least, so it must have happened during the last two hours.

Hell, what kind of bodyguard was he? He hadn't heard a thing. And how the hell had whoever it was avoided the sensor lights?

The light snapped off and he heard Ria hissing loudly as if some mangy cat had invaded her personal space. She was over by the fence separating Emily's house from her neighbor's. Nicholas joined her, squatting down among the plants to see what had upset her.

In the early dawn light, he noticed someone—or something—had flattened the plants up against the fence. A heavy weight, certainly heavier than a cat. The indentation of two footprints—two large footprints—showed up clearly in the soft earth of the garden. At a guess, he'd say a man's size nine ripple-soled shoe, pointed in the direction of the back door.

"Good girl, Ria. Smart cat. You can be my partner any day of the week." He stroked his hand along the animal's back in appreciation before he stood and followed the line their uninvited guest had taken.

He kept his gaze fixed on the sensor lights as he slid along the wall of the house to the back door. Not once did they come on.

"Shit, they're angled too high. He must have come over the fence and crept along close to the house. I'll have to fix them before tonight."

The cat sat at his feet, looking intelligently up at him as if she'd understood every word he'd said. Nicholas shook his head. *How dumb can you get? Standing here talking to a fur-ball.*

He marched toward the open door. Ria followed him, stalking back into the house. Nicholas closed and locked the door before checking the front windows as well. Ria remained in the kitchen, whining and growling.

"What now, cat?"

She raced to the corner of the room and proceeded to howl her displeasure, glaring at him with glowing yellow eyes.

"Stupid me." Nicholas tapped his forehead with the heel of his hand. "First you want out. Now you want feeding. You're not going to wait for anyone, are you?"

He paused, as if expecting the cat to answer. Shaking his head at his own foolishness, he turned toward the refrigerator to retrieve the can of cat food, wrinkling his nose at the pungent odor. Ria backed off while he filled her plate. The moment he'd finished, she butted his hand out of the way to get to the mashed-up fish.

"This is no way to start the day," Nicholas mumbled as he left the kitchen and stomped up the staircase to the bedroom. If he were lucky, he'd still get a couple of hours' sleep before he had to get up again.

Emily had curled up on her side, the covers pulled over her shoulder. During the time he'd been outside with Ria, she'd managed to kick the pillow barrier onto the floor. Nicholas tried to ignore the fact that there was now nothing separating them.

Holding his breath, he eased into bed, making a concerted effort not to disturb his sleeping bed-partner. Stretching, he rested his arms on the pillow above his head, let out a heartfelt sigh and closed his eyes, praying for some much-needed rest.

The edges of his consciousness were beginning to dim when Emily suddenly moved. He didn't pay too much attention at first. She was a restless sleeper. He'd found that out when he'd been lying there watching her during the night. She'd settle down in a few seconds.

His whole body jerked in reaction when she cuddled into him. He held himself stiffly, waiting for her to roll away again.

She didn't.

She moved nearer, pressing her scantily clad body close. Her head came to rest on his chest, dark hair spreading out, brushing his skin like strands of soft silk. The floral-scented perfume of her shampoo rose to meet him, awakening his libido. Hell, he wasn't certain it had even been asleep. He'd been tied in knots since he'd met Ms. Emily Payne.

One small hand walked its way up his chest and came to a halt just beneath his chin. If he lowered his head a fraction, he'd be able to brush her knuckles with his lips. He resisted the impulse, gritted his teeth and waited. Surely she'd roll away in a minute?

It was wishful thinking. She snuggled closer, one long, slim leg coming to rest across his lower body. Now she was sprawled half over him, the soft cushion of her breasts pressing into his chest. He groaned, wondering what the hell he was going to do now. How the devil was a man supposed to sleep when a gorgeous woman like Emily treated him like her favorite toy?

He knew he should move her back to her side of the bed, but he couldn't. Ethics be dammed, he wanted—no, needed—this stolen interlude. Needed to hold her just for a short time, to pretend this was more than a job. He gave in to the clamoring of his body, lowered his hands and hugged her tight, running his palms over the black lace of her teddy.

Closing his eyes, he groaned. This was like having all his fantasies rolled up in one tight little package called Emily Payne and just for the moment, she was his.

Time enough in the stark light of day to remember he'd been assigned to guard her, body and soul. He rationalized his actions with the thought that he *was* guarding her body. The manual said nothing about how close the agent had to be—or not be—to the body. He chose to ignore the little imp inside his brain that kept reminding him the first rule an agent learns is never to get emotionally involved with the subject.

ജ്ഷ

Emily woke by degrees, slowly becoming more conscious of the world around her. First, she luxuriated in the warmth that wrapped about her like a heavy cloak. A spicy scent wafted up, confusing her for a moment until she realized it was the smell of Nicholas's aftershave. The pillow under her cheek was hard, resisting all her efforts to mold it into a more comfortable shape when she moved her head. She opened her eyes a fraction and saw bronze flesh where her snowy pillow should have been.

She was sprawled half over Nicholas. No wonder she'd felt so warm. One of his large hands rested high on her hip. The other held her hand tight under his chin. Her cheek rested on the heavily muscled chest she'd admired earlier and her leg was trapped between his. There was no way she could remove it without waking him.

Wow, Emily, you wanted to get close to the man, but this is ridiculous. I mean, how much closer can a person get?

Embarrassment washed over her in a hot wave, her immediate response to pull away. She hesitated, a grin pulling at her lips. Hell, no! Why not take advantage of the situation? It was one sure-fire way to see if he reacted to her.

Conniving? Manipulating? Oh yeah, but even without her self-imposed project to initiate Nicholas into the pleasures of loving a woman, she didn't think she had the strength to deny herself this moment.

Her head told her this was wrong. Her body hungered to be close to this man and her heart... Ah, her heart wanted so much more than the mere physical. Nothing had ever felt so...so right. And just how corny was that? She'd only known him a little over twenty-four hours.

She gently disengaged her hand from his grasp and eased herself up the bed, dragging her leg up between his, closer to the apex of his thighs. He started to stir as soon as she moved. When he opened his eyes, she grinned. "Good morning, Nicholas."

Dropping a quick kiss on his parted lips, she pulled back and looked down at him, ready to make a smart quip about what a terrific teddy bear he made. Her gaze trapped by his, she paused.

The silence in the room was absolute. She felt as if she were drowning in a sea of sensation, caught in the smoldering depths of his dark eyes. Without conscious thought, she allowed her hand to creep up and caress the strong jaw.

She gently ran the pad of her thumb around the outline of his mouth before brushing her fingers up over his cheek. She circled his ear, smiling slightly when he shivered. “You’ve had your ear pierced. How come you don’t wear an earring?”

“I don’t wear—”

“I know,” she interrupted. “You don’t wear one when you’re all dressed up in your suit for work. But you’re on assignment now. I’ll give you one of mine later. I have just the thing.”

She continued her exploration, threading her fingers through his dark hair. Brushing back the lock that had fallen forward over his forehead. Marveling at the texture, the softness. “You have lovely hair. Have you ever thought about having it curled? Men do today, you know. Particularly men like you. You know, gay men.”

Terrific, Emily. The last thing she wanted to do was remind him he was supposed to be gay. She wanted him to get closer to her, not push her away because he suddenly remembered she was the wrong sex.

Before he could respond to her words, she lowered her head and stole another kiss, hoping to divert his thoughts. Nicholas groaned, the sound half bitten off. His hand clenched on her hip. He held his body stiff, as if to avoid reacting to her.

Hah, not likely. She hadn’t come this far to give up now.

When she traced the shape of his lips with the tip of her tongue, he appeared to lose the battle. A guttural growl rippled from his throat. His hands tightened on her hips. She angled the trapped leg higher, pushing against the hard bulge tenting the front of his boxers.

As she opened her mouth on his, he darted his tongue forward to taste. Heat slammed into her, as if the blood in her veins had turned to molten lava. Sensation overwhelmed her. Hunger made her tremble. Hips thrusting forward, she rubbed the swollen lips of her pussy against his leg, trying to find relief from the throbbing ache centered between her thighs.

He suddenly rolled them over. Now Emily lay beneath him, his chest pinning her down and holding her a willing captive. She groaned in frustration when he kept his lower body away from her, one leg thrown across her to keep her from turning toward him.

Emily struggled to catch her breath. Perspiration broke out on her forehead. What had started as an innocent kiss quickly caught fire.

Get real, Emily, there was nothing innocent about that kiss. She had deliberately set out to tease him. Now she got to reap the benefits. Deal with the consequences. Pay the piper. She ran out of clichés as her thought processes shut down and she rode on a tidal wave of pure emotion.

It really was fire. White-hot feelings raced through her blood as he teased her, his tongue delving deep, establishing a rhythm that awoke an echo deep in the core of her. She forgot about everything but the touch of his lips.

First feather-soft, nipping at the fullness of her lower lip. The pressure of his mouth increased, the thrust of his tongue a sweet torment. It swept her along until her heart thumped so hard it was a wonder it didn't bounce right out of her chest.

Nicholas slid one hand up to caress her breast and she almost lost the ability to breathe altogether. The lace barrier of her teddy created an erotic friction under his palm. Her nipples tightened into throbbing points. When he took the hardened tip, lace and all, into the warmth of his mouth and suckled hard, the air gusted from her lungs in a series of needy sobs. The tug of his mouth generated a flash of heat from her breasts right down to her core.

Nicholas slipped his leg between hers, applying a subtle pressure against the swollen lips of her sex. Tension coiled tight in her belly. Her internal muscles clenched, flooding her pussy with creamy moisture. The crotch of her teddy grew wet and an ache started deep inside. Oh God, she wanted him so bad...stretching her...filling her...until she climaxed around him. And she had no doubts Nicholas wanted her, too.

She'd have to be a moron not to be aware of his desire. With a ragged groan, he ground himself against her, his rigid cock nudging her upper thigh. Almost sobbing with the need to release the tension spiraling out of control inside her, she spread her legs and tried to pull him over her.

He resisted. She slid her hands inside the elastic band of his boxers to clench at taut buttocks as muscled as the rest of him. Tightening her grip, she tried again. "Nicholas," she whimpered.

The sound of her voice broke the spell. Nicholas stilled, staring down at her, eye wide open, a look of chagrin flashing across his face.

"Hell, I'm sorry, Emily. I don't... I can't—"

Suddenly he jerked away from her. Rearing up, he swung his legs over the side of the bed and reached for his jeans and tee shirt. Clutching his clothes, he left the room faster than she would have believed possible. When she heard the bathroom door slam, she shook her head in bewilderment.

Frustration clawed at her insides. She struggled to calm her racing heart and fragmented breathing. "Oh freakin' hell, why did I open my big mouth? All I did was remind him I'm the wrong gender. Now he's probably feeling guilty because he responded to me. And he *did* respond. Some things can't be faked."

She sat up among the rumpled sheets and pushed her hair back from her face. Her body, denied release, was drawn tight as a bowstring. She wrapped her arms about her and waited.

The sound of water running in the bathroom ceased and a few minutes later, Nicholas entered the bedroom, his face wiped clean of all expression. He moved over to the bed, slid his hand under his pillow and pulled out the Glock hidden beneath.

Emily hadn't even known she'd been sleeping with a gun in the bed. She watched in silence while he slipped the weapon into the pancake holster attached to his belt and snuggled into the small of his back. Then he pulled open the top drawer the bedside table, retrieved his back-up weapon and strapped it to his ankle, pulling his jeans down to cover it. It was patently obvious he was avoiding eye contact and he still hadn't said a word. Wasn't he ever going to talk again?

"Nicholas, I don't—"

"I'll go down and start on breakfast," he interrupted. "I'll leave you to get dressed."

Within a heartbeat, he was gone and Emily was alone with her thoughts.

"You stupid, stupid fool," she whispered. "What have you done? Why did you initiate that kiss? Now he can't even look at you."

ഇഅ

Emily placed the magnifying glass gently on the desk and flexed her fingers to work out the stiffness. “Enough already. I’ll go cross-eyed if I keep looking at these little squiggles much longer.”

She peered at the small piece of papyrus. Only two more lines to translate. She’d be glad to get it finished.

No, she wouldn’t, because completing the translation meant Nicholas would leave. There’d be no reason for him to remain here with her. The thought depressed her, filling her with a sense of loneliness.

He’d hardly spoken to her since he’d bolted out of bed this morning. How was she supposed to get close to the man when he couldn’t stand to be in the same room with her?

What started as curiosity, a project, had suddenly become much more. How had it happened? It wasn’t just sex, although, heaven forbid, she could handle some of that, too. Was it just ego? A chance to prove her point?

No, it was more than that. Nicholas had become important to her. She almost felt as if she’d found the other half of herself. The balance she needed to make her life whole. Dare she say it? Her soul mate?

The problem was, how did she convince Nicholas he needed her? And what would she do if it turned out he were truly gay?

She knew she couldn’t work any more. Her mind was too full of thoughts of her reluctant houseguest. Gathering up her translations and the papyrus, she eased them back into the protective plastic sleeve. She’d work on it later.

Or maybe she wouldn’t.

The faster she finished the translation, the faster Nicholas would leave and the less chance she’d have to show him they could be good together. A deep sigh feathered across her lips. How did she get herself into these situations?

Picking up the plastic bag, she left the office. She'd go down and see what Nicholas was doing, but first she had to collect a few things from the bedroom. She had an experiment to conduct. One she hoped would go a long way toward showing her whether her guest was what he said he was.

Chapter Six

"Can you lock that away for me? I've had enough for the moment."

Nicholas jumped as the plastic sleeve containing the papyrus and Emily's translation sailed over his shoulder to land on the couch beside him. He made a move to stand, intent on locking the papyrus in the safe, but Emily was too quick for him.

"No, not yet. Do it later. I want to check something else first."

She ran her fingers through his thick hair, nails scraping along his scalp. Nicholas shivered, tensing as he fought to damp down the wave of intense sexual energy sweeping through him.

"Hmm. Yes, it should be long enough."

He sighed with disappointment when she removed her hand.

She rounded the couch and dropped an armful of items on the cushion beside him. He stared at them. Comb. Hairbrush. Hairspray. Mousse. Heated rollers.

Oh, no, she wouldn't... She couldn't... Could she?

Before he gathered his scattered wits and put up a protest, Emily grabbed the container of heated rollers and plugged them into the power socket beside the television. Dropping onto her knees in front of him, she wedged herself between his spread thighs.

When she placed her hands high on his denim-clad legs, he gulped. His heart sped up and a surge of hunger engulfed his body. Heat shafted through him, driving the blood downward to fill his cock. If she moved her hands another inch she'd cop a feel of the rock-hard boner straining at the front of his jeans. He wanted to grab hold of her and pull her close. Taste the sweetness of her mouth again. Lose himself—

Biting off a groan, he clamped down on the licentious thoughts swirling through his brain. He couldn't get involved. Emily was a "for-keeps" kind of woman, the sort a man couldn't walk away from. He wasn't ready for that type of commitment.

Liar, whispered the little voice inside his mind. He chose to ignore it. He was a rough, tough federal agent. He'd been trained to handle the worst dregs of human society. Surely he could handle his own libido? He was strong enough to keep this situation under control.

Yeah right, he thought as Emily leaned closer.

"I've found the perfect earring for you. Well, actually, I *was* looking for a very macho skull-and-cross-bones one I had, but I seem to have misplaced it. I had to hunt for something else. This one's perfect 'cause you're so sweet for looking after me."

As she lifted her hand, he spotted the earring hanging from her fingers. A bright red love-heart about the size of his thumbnail dangled from a silver chain attached to a silver stud.

A shudder ripped through him. Fucking hell, she wanted him to wear that? He'd look like a right charlie. Everyone would think he was gay. Yeah, right, everyone—including Emily—and he couldn't tell her any different. At least, not yet.

He couldn't tell her he'd had his ear pierced last year as part of his disguise in a special undercover operation. Once the job was over, he'd removed the stud, hoping the hole would close up. And now she wanted to hang a ridiculous heart off his lobe? Like hell.

"Emily, I don't think—"

"Oh, stop fussing, Nicholas. It'll look terrific. No one is going to see it but me so why worry?"

She leaned even closer and reached for his ear. Goosebumps broke out on his flesh at her touch. As she slid the stud through his lobe and pushed the butterfly clip home to keep the earring in place, her perfume curled about him, awakening every little testosterone gremlin in his body.

He shook his head and the little red heart swung against his neck. He was amazed he hadn't put up a better fight. Shit, he'd sat there like a freakin' idiot and let her have her way with him. Man, he had it bad.

"Okay, the rollers should be hot enough now." She unplugged them and moved around to the back of the couch.

"Ah, hang on, Emily. This is a joke, right? You're not going to do this, are you?"

"Of course I am. Why else would I heat the rollers?"

"But I like my hair straight. I did what Mom said and ate all my crusts when I was a kid and it's still straight, just the way it was meant to be. I really don't think I want to do this."

Nicholas couldn't believe this was happening to him. His immediate reaction was to get the hell out of there as fast as possible. He even went so far as tensing his muscles, ready to bolt. Then he slumped against the backrest of the couch. Damn it, he was supposed to be gay.

His brother was gay and he regularly permed his hair. If that's what was necessary to maintain his cover, he'd just have to sit and take it like a man. He crossed his arms and released a long-suffering sigh.

"Don't fuss so much, Nicholas. I think you'll look terrific with curls. Sort of like a modern day Byron. You don't happen to write poetry, do you?"

Emily sent up a silent prayer he'd object as strongly as any normal heterosexual male would to having his hair curled. She waited a moment to see if he'd do anything about it then sighed. Damn! Looked like it wasn't going to happen.

When no further objections were forthcoming, she parted his hair into segments and started to wind the rollers around each clump, securing them with thin metal pins. "Pass me up another roller," she mumbled, watching for any reaction as she sectioned off the hair above his right ear.

The experiment was not going the way she'd hoped it would. If Nicholas were straight, surely he would have put up more of a fight? She swallowed her disappointment, mentally shrugging. All projects needed time. Time to assess, to evaluate, to allow all the various parts to come together in a natural conclusion. This project was no different. She just had to be patient.

Tilting her head to one side, she surveyed her handiwork. "Yes, I think curls will look great on you. Of course, if you don't like it when I've finished, we can wash it out."

She slid another pin home. "You know, lots of guys curl their hair nowadays and some of them are even staunch heterosexuals. Surely you've come into contact with other gay men who curl and color their hair?" She paused a moment, in the process of fastening the next roller. "Now there's a thought. I think I've got some peroxide in the bathroom cupboard. We could give you blond tips."

"*Forget it.*" Nicholas tried to jump up from the couch, only to have Emily pull him back again.

"Oh, stop being such a baby. I promise I won't alter the color of your hair."

She dropped the comb over his shoulder into his lap. "There. All finished. Now we wait five minutes for the rollers to cool a bit. After that, I'll brush you out. In the meantime, I'll go make a coffee."

Nicholas shook his head, grimacing at the unaccustomed weight of the rollers. He was tempted to get up and have a look in the mirror over the fireplace. Nah. Maybe not. He wasn't certain he could stand the sight.

Why the hell had he allowed himself to get talked into this? But then, he hadn't. Allowed himself to get talked into it, that is. Hell, he was even starting to sound like Emily.

She was like a fierce tornado, catching up everything and everyone in her path. Before he knew where he was, he was calmly sitting there letting her curl his hair. He'd turned into a wimp. This had to stop.

"Here you go. You drink that while I take the rollers out. We really should wait until they're completely cool, but this will at least give us an idea of how it'll look. We can always redo it all again later."

"Not fucking likely," Nicholas murmured under his breath. He grabbed for the cup of hot coffee as she passed it over the back of the couch. Knowing his luck, she'd drop it in his lap if he weren't careful.

She started unwinding the rollers, running her fingers through the loosened curls. "You know, you never did tell me when you came to the conclusion you were gay."

Nicholas groaned. Ah, crap, she was at it again. She simply wouldn't leave the subject alone. He didn't want to lie to her any more than he already had so he kept his mouth shut.

"It's just that you don't really seem comfortable with your sexual orientation. It's as if it's all new to you. That's why I wondered if it were a recent thing." She whipped out another roller and dropped it on the couch.

A heavy knocking sounded on the front door. Nicholas was glad for the interruption. At least it put an end to Emily's speculations. Before he could do anything about it, Emily moved to the front window and twitched the curtain aside.

"Emily, get away from the window."

"It's okay. It's Marty."

Nicholas tried to place the coffee cup on the low table in front of him and untangle his long legs at the same time. He managed to get the cup down without spilling anything, but tripped over his own feet, falling to his knees.

"Don't open the freakin' door," he yelled again as he pushed himself upright and bolted after Emily.

Damn, would the woman never learn? She had to get into the habit of letting him do things first. It was Marty this time, but it could well be the person bent on stealing the papyrus next time.

He groaned as he suddenly remembered he hadn't locked the papyrus away. He was getting as ditzy as Emily. The papyrus was still on the couch among a welter of hair rollers, brushes and combs. He groaned even louder when he thought of Marty's reaction to his curly hair. Just his luck. He'd never live this down.

"Agent Tomlins, how nice to see you."

"Miss Emily," he greeted her. "I've brought you some groceries. I didn't know what you liked so I just chose a selection. Lots of red meat, too. I know old Nick likes his steak."

"I'm sure whatever you have there will be fine, Agent Tomlins." Emily guided him in and closed the door behind him.

"Call me Marty. Everyone does."

"Only if you drop the miss and just call me plain Emily."

"No one could ever call you plain, Emily. You're one sexy lady." Marty bowed gallantly from the waist.

Nicholas had had enough. Marty Tomlins was old enough to be Emily's father and here he was, flirting with her. What the fuck did he think he was doing?

He cleared his throat, dragging the other agent's attention away from Emily. "How about you take those through to the kitchen, Marty. It's down the hallway on your left."

Marty spun around to face him, his eyes widening in shock, his face contorting as if he were in severe pain. What the hell was wrong with the man?

Nicholas suddenly slapped a hand over the front of his hair as if he could hide the evidence of his foolishness. He didn't need to be told what was wrong with Marty. He knew. It was the sight of the Agency heartthrob, big macho Nick, standing there with rollers in his hair.

He struggled to rip the two remaining curlers out, but all he managed to do was get them tangled. No matter how hard he pulled, they wouldn't budge.

"Not one word, Tomlins. Not one word," he warned as he fought with the knotted rollers.

"Nicholas, leave them alone," Emily remonstrated. "You'll tangle it even more and I'll have to cut them out."

She grabbed him by the arm and led him back to the living room. After she'd pushed him onto the couch, she went to work on the tangled rollers.

Marty followed them into the room a few moments later, minus the groceries. "Nice look you have there, Nick, my friend," he said as he sat down. His mouth twitched and he started to laugh.

"Marty," Nicholas warned again in an ominous tone of voice.

"I don't believe it," Marty gasped when he could catch his breath. "I never thought I'd see the day." Still wheezing with laughter, he jumped up and left the room.

Nicholas breathed a sigh of relief when he heard the front door open. He'd expected more of a razzing. He was amazed he'd been let off so lightly. Then he knew he hadn't been. Marty entered the house again, talking ten to the dozen to someone else, his sentences punctuated with laughter.

"I told you so," Marty said as he entered the living room with Terry Banks in tow.

Nicholas dropped his head into his hands. It was no use. It'd be around the Agency in no time flat now. Terry Banks and Marty Tomlins were the biggest gossips in the department.

Terry burst out laughing. "If I hadn't seen it with my own eyes, I wouldn't have believed it," he spluttered. "Oh, Nicky, darling, you look beautiful. I love the new hairstyle. It's so you."

"Hey, leave him alone, you two," Emily piped up. "I think he looks fine."

Nicholas winced as Emily dragged the brush roughly through his new curls. For fuck's sake, this couldn't be happening to him. The guys would never let him forget this.

Terry minced across the room, swinging his hips in an exaggerated arc. "Why, Nicky," he lisped in a falsetto voice. "I do love the new earring. Red hearts really go with the curly look. Have you got a date yet for tonight, love?"

"I didn't know you were gay, too, Agent Banks," Emily chimed in.

Suddenly, Terry Banks wasn't laughing any longer. He backed up, hands held in front of him as if to ward off some imagined enemy.

The look of horror on Terry's face was so comical Nicholas couldn't help himself. Now it was his turn to laugh. Emily didn't know it, but she'd just turned the tables for him. *Let's see how Terry gets out of this one.*

"I'm not gay," Terry spluttered. "I'm as straight as...as straight as—"

"As Nicholas is?" Marty quipped on another wave of hilarity.

Emily struggled to keep her face straight. "Terry, I'm confused. I thought I heard you ask Nicholas on a date for tonight." She knew Terry wasn't gay, but he worked so hard at being the professional agent, she couldn't help but try to prick his bubble a little bit.

"No, it wasn't a date," Terry snapped.

"But I heard you."

"It wasn't a date. I was just fooling around," Terry all but yelled.

Nicholas surged to his feet, swept his hand through his dark curls, and sauntered over to Terry. As she watched him place his arm around Terry's shoulders and hug him, Emily's heart dropped down into her boots.

"Ah, come on, Terry, love," Nicholas said in a sickly-sweet, high voice, not at all like his normal macho tone. "It's okay if Emily knows. After all, Marty told her *I* was gay. She's not going to think any less of you if you admit it. But I think we'd better give the date a miss tonight. I have to stay here and guard Emily. Maybe after the case is over."

Emily's brain was having trouble assimilating the information it was being fed. For the first time, she saw Nicholas acting as if he really were gay. She knew he was teasing Terry, but what if the rest of it wasn't an act?

"I'm out of here." Terry disengaged himself from Nicholas's hold and stomped out of the house, the door slamming behind him.

Nicholas and Marty collapsed on the couch, laughing so hard they were gasping for breath.

Emily couldn't see anything funny in the situation. A black cloud of depression descended on her. Deep in her heart she'd convinced herself Nicholas really wasn't gay. That he simply hadn't met the right woman. Until her, that is.

Now she found it hard to refute the evidence of her own eyes, and if Nicholas were gay, what she was doing in trying to convert him was wrong. It would be better if she forgot her personal project. Better for Nicholas. Better for her.

Her mind firmly made up, she left the two men in the living room and wandered into the kitchen, trying not to allow the depression to take over.

After all, it was her own fault. Marty had told her Nicholas was gay. It wasn't his problem if she found him wildly attractive. It wasn't his fault her heart beat faster every time he was near. He hadn't set out to hurt her.

She'd done that all on her own.

ຈາຄ

Emily retrieved the papyrus from where it still sat on the living room couch and retreated to her office. She may as well try to finish the translation. The sooner she finished, the sooner Nicholas would leave.

She knew she was being contrary. Earlier, she'd wanted to delay completion of the translation to keep Nicholas with her. Now she realized it was better for her peace of mind if he left quickly. Before she got used to having him around.

Too late. The words echoed loudly in her brain.

"Oh, shut up," Emily muttered. "I'll get over it. I don't believe in love at first sight. That only happens in the movies."

She chose to ignore the ache in the region of her heart as she tried to immerse herself in her work.

Ten minutes later, she dropped the magnifying glass on the desk and buried her head in her hands. It was no good. She couldn't concentrate. Her mind was too full of thoughts of Nicholas and what might have been. There was no way she'd get any work done feeling like this.

Sliding everything back into the plastic sleeve, she left the office, collecting her purse and glasses from the bedroom before heading back downstairs. Nicholas and Marty were still sitting in the living room talking.

She joined them, handing the plastic bag to Nicholas. Flopping down onto the couch beside Marty, she tucked her legs underneath her. As he locked the papyrus away, Nicholas spoke softly to the Boston fern. Her mouth quirked, but she couldn't raise a proper smile. She felt too down and there was only one thing to do when she got this way.

"I want to go shopping."

There was absolute silence in the room. Anyone would think she'd just announced she'd killed someone.

"Excuse me?" The tone of Nicholas's voice was just short of horrified.

"I want to go shopping."

Nicholas strode across to her, every inch the serious, professional agent. When he laid his hand on her shoulder, Emily flinched. She didn't want him to touch her. It made her want more than she could have. More than he was capable of giving.

"Emily, you can't go out. We can't leave the papyrus here. Not now we definitely know someone is trying to break into the house."

"Who tried to break into the house?" Emily stared at him, her forehead pulled down into a frown. "When?"

"I didn't want to worry you, but someone tried to force your back door last night. I found the evidence this morning. Or at least Ria did."

Nicholas ran his hand through his hair, ruffling the curls Emily had so carefully created. "Why do you want to go shopping now? Marty has stocked the pantry. There's no need to go out."

"I'm just too... Oh, I don't know." Emily shrugged. She couldn't tell him she was too depressed because she'd realized there was no future for them. "I can't work. I'm too keyed up. Restless. And the only solution when I'm like this is to go shopping."

"But what about the papyrus? We can't leave the house unprotected. Anyone with the knowledge and expertise would crack that safe in a minute." He held up his hand as Emily opened her mouth to speak. "And you can't go wandering around on your own. You're too important to this project."

"I won't be on my own. I'll have my bodyguard with me. As far as the papyrus goes, we could—"

"We are not going anywhere with that thing tucked inside your bra again, Emily," Nicholas interrupted, frowning at the snort of laughter, quickly smothered, that came from Marty.

"There's our answer." Emily gestured to Marty. She sat down beside him and laid a hand on his arm. "Marty, will you stay and guard the house? Pretty please, Marty? I really need to get out for a while."

She hated to beg, but she wasn't lying when she'd said she needed to get out. She felt a tad claustrophobic with all the doors and windows shut tight. It made the atmosphere of the house too intimate, too close.

"Can't see why not." Marty grinned, patting her hand. "We were assigned to this case to watch the house once Nicholas reported the attempted break-in. There's no reason why I can't watch the house from the inside."

"Thank you, Marty." Emily smiled at him before turning to Nicholas. "So can we go? I don't want to go far, just down to the Five Ways here in Paddington. We could even walk there."

"All right, all right. I give up. We'll go shopping. Marty will look after the house. But we won't be walking. That puts you too much at risk."

"It's not me they want. It's the papyrus."

"They'd still need you to translate it. No, if we're going, we drive."

"Get Terry to take you in the Agency car," Marty piped up. "It's bigger than yours. Emily might need the extra space after she's been shopping. If she's anything like my wife, she'll arrive home with a stack of things she doesn't really need."

Nicholas had never been shopping with a woman, but he'd heard the married men from the agency gripe about taking their partners shopping. He wasn't looking forward to this.

"Okay, Marty, you let the control officer know what's going on, while we get ready."

"I *am* ready." Emily grabbed her purse off the couch where she'd dropped it.

Nicholas halted on the verge of leaving the room. He turned and ran his gaze over Emily's brightly clad body. Today she sported a bright blue gathered skirt with pink splotches all over it. She'd teamed it with a deep purple singlet top with yellow ducks marching across her chest.

"Um, Emily, are you going out like that?"

"What's wrong with it? I'm fully covered."

"Ah, it's a bit bright." Nicholas hesitated, not wanting to hurt her feelings. "I take it you dressed without your glasses this morning?"

"Maybe the skirt's too much." She frowned. "No problems. I'll get rid of it."

As she casually started to unzip her skirt, Nicholas's mouth dropped open. Surely she wasn't going to change here, right in front of Marty? He suddenly felt a shaft of jealousy spear his heart. Married or not, he didn't want any other man getting his fill of those long, tapering legs hidden by the voluptuous folds of bright blue fabric.

"Ah, Emily, shouldn't you... Marty might..."

His words trailed off as the skirt slid down and pooled about her feet. He breathed a heart-felt sigh as he realized she had shorts on under the skirt. For crying out loud, who put shorts on under a skirt? *No one else but Emily,* he answered himself. Thankfully, they didn't clash too badly with the purple top.

"There, is that better?" She peered down at the shorts. "I think they're black so they should look all right."

"Actually, they're navy blue, but they'll do." Nicholas grinned. "Wanna tell me why you had both shorts *and* a skirt on today?"

Emily shrugged. "I was going to put in some time in the garden, but this is even better."

He shook his head. He'd never met a woman who cared so little for her appearance. It was refreshing. Most of the women he'd dated kept a man waiting for hours while they readied themselves to go out. This was a real change, one he rather liked. There was something about going for spontaneity, rather than planning everything down to the last detail.

"Okay, if we're going, let's get this show on the road."

Lifting up the cushion on one of the lounge chairs, he grabbed the Glock he'd hidden there earlier, just to keep it close to hand. "Give me a minute to grab a holster and I'll be back."

Taking the stairs two at a time, he rushed into the bedroom and pulled a shoulder holster out of his bag. His denim jacket was too short to wear the pancake holster. This would have to do. He fitted it on and settled it in place, sliding the weapon home and checking it was secure. He shrugged into the jacket and joined the others in the living room.

"Nicholas, it's too hot to wear a jacket."

"Sorry, but it's standard dress when one wears a gun and holster. The general public might get spooked if they knew I carried. Now let's get out of here."

He offered his arm to Emily and guided her out into the hallway, Marty following them.

"Ah, Nick," Marty interrupted. "I think Emily looks great, but are *you* going like that?"

Nicholas halted and turned back to face Marty. "What on earth are you talking about?"

Marty extended his hand and gently flicked the earring dangling from his lobe. The red love heart bumped against the side of his neck. Nicholas felt himself flushing with embarrassment. He'd totally forgotten about the stupid earring.

He quickly undid the little butterfly clip holding it in place and removed it. Sliding the backing and the love heart into his top pocket, he ran his hand through his hair. Crap, it was still full of fluffy little curls.

Well, there was nothing he could do about it right now. No way would the curls comb out. He'd have to wash his hair to get rid of them and he didn't think Emily would wait that long. He prayed he didn't run into anyone else he knew. The boys would dine out on this for the next century as it was.

He ushered Emily outside and over to the blue vehicle parked on the opposite side of the street. Terry Banks jumped out of the car as he saw them approach.

"Emily wants to go shopping," Nicholas said. "And you're the designated driver."

Terry didn't say anything. Instead, he gave Emily a cautious look and opened the back door, slamming it closed after them.

When he slid in behind the steering wheel, Emily leaned forward so she could talk to him. "Do you know where the Five Ways Shopping Center is, Terry?"

"Yeah, I was raised not far from here so I know this area quite well. I'll have you there in a jiffy."

"Great. I haven't been on a shopping spree in ages. This is long overdue." She sat back and buckled her belt. "Although I still think it would have been easier to walk."

Within minutes, they'd arrived and Terry had parked the car. When Emily made a move to get out of the vehicle, Nicholas pulled her back and insisted on going first. Emily slid out behind him while he stood there surveying the line of shops.

"Where to first?"

"Oh, didn't I tell you? We're only going to one shop. There. That one."

Nicholas looked across the street to where Emily pointed. One name, in bright fluorescent pink, stood out above all the others.

Delectable Delights.

His eyes opened wide as he took in the display in the window. Oh, she wouldn't.

"Ah, Emily, that's... That's a ladies'..." His voice failed him.

"Yes, I know what it is. This is what I do when I get down. I go shopping for sexy underwear."

Chapter Seven

"You can't be serious." Nicholas groaned, a pained expression on his face.

"Of course I am. This is what I do when I can't work."

"Haven't you got enough? If what I saw last night is a sample of what you have in that top drawer, you have a more than adequate supply. I really don't want to do this. I think we should go back to the house."

Emily frowned as she heard Agent Banks snigger. What was all the fuss about? It was only an underwear store. Okay, so the items for sale were rather on the saucy side, but there was nothing wrong with that. She liked sexy lingerie.

"Look, don't be such a wuss, Nicholas. There's nothing wrong with a man going into a lingerie shop. Men take their partners shopping all the time."

"I do my shopping on my own and I certainly don't do it in shops like that one."

"They sell menswear as well. If it worries you, pretend you're looking at those. If it really upsets you, you can stand outside and wait for me."

"You know I can't do that. I'm your bodyguard."

"Sorry, Nicholas, you'll just have to guard this body from inside the store. Now come on, let's go."

Emily grabbed Nicholas by the arm and frog-marched him down the street to the store. She hoped this trip was worth it. She really needed a lift to her spirits. She may have to accept he was gay, but did he have to make it so plain he didn't want to go shopping with her?

Her spirits plummeted even further. She tried to ignore the little voice reminding her this was none of Nicholas's doing. She'd been told he was gay right from the outset. It was her own fault her emotions were a bit battered, but she'd get over it. She had to. There was obviously no chance of a relationship between them so she had no choice. And she'd start by enjoying her shopping spree.

When they entered the store, she left Nicholas standing near the exit while she wandered through the racks of brightly colored sleepwear. She didn't really need any more nightgowns. She had plenty at home. Come to that, she didn't need any new underwear either. But going shopping made her feel good, and besides, she loved sensual, sexy satins and silks against her skin.

Emily selected a matching set of top and French knickers in black with bright red lips printed on the fabric. Wandering over to another rack, she pulled out a bodysuit in ivory satin and lace.

She'd turned toward the fitting rooms when she spotted a cami-bra and suspender bikini set teamed with romantic lace-top stockings. Heaven knew when she'd wear it, but something about it appealed. After finding the right size, she hugged her bounty to her chest and marched toward the fitting rooms.

Nicholas started after her only to have the saleswoman stop him.

"Sir, you can't go in there."

"Sorry, ma'am, but I have to—"

"This is the ladies' fitting room. I can't allow you to go in there."

Nicholas ran his hand through his hair, grimaced again at the fluffy curls and released a long sigh of impatience. Would nothing go right this day? Silently counting to ten to control his annoyance, he faced down the saleswoman.

"Once again, I'm sorry, but I have to go in there with this woman." He looked around, but Emily had gone, swallowed up by the heavy folds of curtain covering the entrance to the fitting room. She could at least have waited until he'd sorted this out.

"And *I'm* sorry, but I repeat, you cannot go in there." The woman raised one eyebrow, giving his a supercilious look. "If you're going to argue about this, I'll have to call the supervisor."

"So call the supervisor because I'm going in there right now." He pointed in the general direction of the fitting rooms.

"No sir, you are not. The men's changing rooms are on the other side of the shop if you need them."

"I don't want to try anything on," he said in frustration. "I just need…"

His voice strangled in his throat and died away as Emily pulled aside the curtain and stood framed in the doorway. His jaw dropped and his eyes opened wide.

His body tightened with desire as his gaze skimmed over her. She had changed into one of the outfits she'd chosen. It was a little baby-doll top with shoestring straps. The lower edge of the top stopped just shy of her waist. The only thing holding it together was a black satin bow tantalizingly positioned between her breasts.

The heat increased as he lowered his gaze. The matching knickers were so high at the sides, nothing but an elastic band and a frill of black lace riding high on her hipbone marred the smooth sweep of her long legs.

The fabric itself finally caught his attention. Shiny, slinky satin in deepest black. It was the red lips frozen in a pouty kiss that had him fixated. He wanted to get down on his knees and press his lips to each and every one of those kiss marks.

"Miss, you can't come out here like that," the shop assistant remonstrated, her tone scandalized.

"Hey, I'm covered and I wasn't about to come *all* the way out into the shop. I just wanted Nicholas's opinion."

Only just covered, Nicholas thought as he swallowed hard through a throat gone suddenly dry and raspy. "Um, Emily, maybe you should go back inside and change. You never know what weirdo could be lurking around a place like this."

The shop assistant drew herself up to her full height. "Sir, we don't have any of those type of people around here, lurking or not."

"Well, you do have one," Emily interrupted. "The guy peering in the window." Pulling the curtain up to hide her attire, she gestured over Nicholas's shoulder to the display window at the front of the store.

Both Nicholas and the saleswoman spun about to look at the window. *And* the man with his face pressed hard against the glass.

Regardless of the heat of mid-summer, he was dressed in a thick overcoat with the collar pulled up high around the lower half of his face. On his head was a floppy gray felt hat, the brim tugged down to shadow his face. When he realized he was the center of attention, he quickly moved away from the window and disappeared.

Nicholas tensed and then relaxed. It was probably just a peeping Tom, or maybe a flasher, but he still felt an instant of disquiet. It took him a few minutes to realize it wasn't just the case, but the thought of another man seeing Emily dressed, or rather, undress as she was at the moment.

Annoyed with his lack of professionalism, he took her by the arm and practically shoved her into the fitting room. "Get dressed."

"I haven't finished trying on the other outfits."

"Well, get on with it and we can get out of here," he growled as he started to follow Emily.

"Sir, I told you, you cannot go in there." The saleswoman stood in front of him, hands on hips, a belligerent look on her face.

Emily intervened. "It's okay. He has to come with me. He's my bodyguard."

"But what if the other customers object?" the woman protested.

Emily ducked her head behind the curtain. "Hey, do any of you women mind if a gorgeous, sexy male comes into the dressing area? He's just going to stand here in the corridor." She tugged Nicholas by the hand through the curtained doorway.

Small cubicles lined the side of the area, each screened from view by a floral curtain. Nicholas squirmed as a feminine face appeared from behind each drape, all of them peering at him. A rush of heat flooded his face as they gave him the once-over. One woman even went so far as to leave the cubical and waltz over to him, clad only in a white lace bra and matching panties. She moved in close and ran a red-tipped fingernail down his cheek.

"Honey, you can come and watch me change anytime you like. Right, girls?" she whispered in a sultry voice.

There was an immediate chorus of affirmation from the rest of the women.

"This is highly irregular," the saleswoman remonstrated, throwing her hands into the air as she walked away.

Nicholas ignored her comment and leaned up against the wall, eyeballing the curtain Emily had disappeared behind. Damn it, he wished she'd hurry. He couldn't remember any other time in his life when he'd felt so uncomfortable.

Just then, the curtain swished aside and Emily posed in the opening.

"What do you think, Nicholas? You reckon a normal hetero male would be turned on by this?"

Nicholas stared. He couldn't think of an intelligent word to say. Emily stood there in a black lace bra and panties set. Suspenders hung from the edge of the panties, attached to the lacy tops of sheer black stockings.

It was the type of outfit every man dreamed of seeing his woman wear. He salivated just thinking about Emily coming to him dressed in such an outfit. It took a major effort of his intellectual processes to remind himself she wasn't his woman. Now if only he could get his cock to remember. He straightened, trying to adjust the fit of his jeans so his rock-hard erection wouldn't show.

He had to clear his throat before he could answer. "Um...ah, it's very effective."

"It's called *Sinful Magic*. Do the trick, you think?"

He nodded. It was all he was capable of doing as he watched Emily twist and turn in front of the long mirror at the end of the corridor.

The woman with the blood-red fingernails walked out and approached the mirror. Nicholas rolled his eyes, unable to believe this was happening to him. She was wearing a sheer black number with a band of fur around the hemline. Nothing, but nothing, left to the imagination.

"It looks terrific on your figure, honey," she said, her head cocked on one side as she gave Emily the once-over. "But I'd lose the sneakers if I were you."

Nicholas had to fight hard to keep his face straight. Emily might look as sexy as hell, but she'd spoiled the picture by teaming her fluorescent orange sneakers with the suspenders and black stockings.

"I know we're not normally supposed to try on the stocking, but I'm going to buy them anyway and I wanted to see what they looked like. I didn't want to get a run in them. The sneakers were all I had to put on," Emily tossed over her shoulder as she headed back to the fitting room.

His mouth twitched as he struggled to contain his laughter. He didn't want to offend her. Besides, Emily always looked sexy to him, regardless of what she had on.

Relief washed through him when she disappeared back behind the curtain and he could no longer see that luscious body in the oh-so-sexy outfit. *Sinful Magic* was a good name for it. If he'd been given to poetic ramblings, he would have said he was under some kind of spell, held in thrall by this kooky college professor.

For the first time in his life, he was doing more than giving a passing thought to wedding bells and babies who looked just like Emily, and it scared the crap out of him. It was time to snap out of it. He wasn't the marrying kind. Certainly not with his job. And thinking of his job…

"Can you hurry it up, Emily? I'd like to get out of here."

"Ah, Nicholas, I have a problem."

Emily grimaced. It had been a bit of fun making Nicholas feel uncomfortable while she shopped for underwear, but it was time to go home. And she would...if she could only get her shorts on. Why did the damn zip have to get stuck now?

"What's the problem?" she heard Nicholas ask from the other side of the curtain.

"My zip is stuck and I can't get it free."

"Try tugging it."

She rolled her eyes. "What do you think I've been doing?" Damn it, did he think she was totally thick? She might be a screw-up in most things, but she did know how to dress herself. "It won't budge. You'll have to come in and give me a hand."

There was absolute silence for a moment before Nicholas stepped into the cubicle. His gaze immediately zeroed in on the front of her shorts.

"All right, let me have a go."

Emily sucked in her breath as Nicholas grasped the little metal tab of the zip. It wouldn't have been so bad if it had jammed up near the top. Did it have to happen right at the bottom? Thank heavens she'd worn a decent pair of panties. Nothing too racy. Perfectly plain—if you discounted the black velvet love hearts scattered over the red fabric. She mentally shrugged. At least they weren't see-through.

"I can't get it. Hang on, I'll get down so I can see what I'm doing."

He lowered himself to his knees in front of her. "The fabric's well and truly caught up in the zip. I'll have to try to work it free."

Emily held her breath as Nicholas moved nearer. His dark head was so close to her belly, she had an almost irresistible urge to run her fingers through his hair, to press his face closer. She had to curl her fingers into her palms to stop herself doing something so stupid.

An audible gasp slipped from her mouth as Nicholas fiddled with the fabric just above the stubborn zip. She could have sworn he'd brushed his fingers across one of the furry love hearts. His warm breath feathered across her stomach, seeping through the thin fabric of her panties, making her muscles contract. When he slid his hand into the front of her shorts in an effort to free the snagged material, his knuckles brushed against her mons.

A shiver slithered down Emily's spine. Her heart raced. Heat spiraled through her, coalescing into a raging conflagration centered over her aching clit. God help her, if Nicholas moved his hand much further, he'd be able to feel the creamy dampness of her panties.

She squirmed on the spot, trying to relieve the tension. All without giving in to the urge to grind herself against Nicholas's hand.

"Hey, hold still," Nicholas whispered. "Just a little bit longer and I'll be finished. Don't move an inch."

"Hurry up, Nicholas. I can't stay like this for much longer."

The curtain was suddenly pulled aside and the saleswoman stood in the opening. "Sir, I have to ask you to leave. You, too, madam. We are not that type of establishment."

"Huh? What are you talking about?" Nicholas, his hand still buried in Emily's shorts, frowned up at woman from his position on the floor.

Emily saw the picture as the saleswoman must have viewed it. She started to laugh just as Nicholas managed to free her shorts. As the zip shot home, he fell backward and landed on his ass, his legs sliding between hers. Emily kept laughing, more in relief at the snapping of the tension coiling inside her.

It was some moments before she could compose herself. When she finally caught her breath, she grinned. "She thinks you're down on your knees because you're... Because we are..." She gave up, allowing the laughter to take hold again.

Blotches of red spread across the woman's cheeks. Her mouth was a thin slash of disapproval. When she drew in a shuddering breath and opened her mouth to vent at them again, Emily pulled herself together and tried to explain.

"It's okay. The material got caught in my zip." She nodded to Nicholas. "He was freeing it up for me. Nothing else was going on."

"Oh? Well, it didn't look like that to me. And I'd still like the *gentleman* to leave the fitting area."

Nicholas scrambled to his feet, his face as bright red as the shop assistant's. "Madame, this is not... I'll have you know I'm a respectable federal officer."

"Just vacate the area, sir, before I call security." The woman turned and flounced out of the fitting room.

Emily couldn't help herself. She started to laugh all over again. Nicholas looked so put out, as if someone had maligned his good name. For crying out loud, he was a mature, sophisticated man. He should be able to handle something as simple as a jammed zipper, yet here he was, blushing like a teenager.

The grin still plastered to her face, Emily gathered up her purchases. "Come on, Nicholas, don't get so bent out of shape about it. Surely you've been caught in a compromising position before? It wasn't that bad. She just thinks you were going down on me."

Nicholas's lips started to twitch in the beginnings of a smile. "Let's get out of here before that woman has us arrested for lewd behavior. I'd hate to have to explain this one at the Agency."

Emily followed him out of the fitting area and up to the checkout. Suddenly she turned and shoved the collection of silky garments into his arms. "Keep my place for me. I just have to get a few more things."

As she spun away, Nicholas tried to catch hold of her arm, but she evaded him and dashed across to the menswear section. With a firm idea in her mind as to what she wanted, she zapped around the displays. It wasn't long before she joined Nicholas back at the checkout line, stepping in beside him.

"About time," he whispered. "I'm getting some really weird looks here. These women probably think I'm some sort of pervert or a transvestite shopping for the latest in lingerie."

Emily retrieved her purchases. "Go wait by the door. I'll only be a moment and then we can go home."

She chuckled as he complied with a haste that would have been an insult if it hadn't been so funny. Poor Nicholas. He was out of his element. Shopping for women's underwear wasn't his thing.

Within minutes, she had the new lingerie tucked into a bag with the shop's name emblazoned on the front. When she joined Nicholas, he wasted no time in ushering her out of the store and across the road to the car.

Terry opened the door as they approached. "Have fun, Nick?" he taunted as they climbed into the vehicle. "Shame I couldn't have joined you."

As Nicholas scowled at Terry's teasing, Emily dug into her bag of purchases. Leaning forward, she handed Terry a scrunched up piece of black fabric. "It's all right, Terry. You didn't miss out. I bought you a present."

Terry shook out the garment. As he stared at it, the color leached from his face. Nicholas took one look and burst out laughing, Emily joining him. They weren't that bad. Poor Terry. The look on his face was priceless.

Emily had bought him a pair of black boxers. Functional gift—except for one thing. The fabric was sheer. Totally see-through. The only adornment was a pink velvet bow situated right over the most strategic part of a man's anatomy.

Every time Nicholas looked at them, he burst into another raucous bout of laughter. Emily frowned. Damn it, it wasn't that funny. They were cute. A perfectly respectable pair of boxer shorts. Okay, maybe a bit kinky, she conceded, but it was all just a bit of fun. Wait until Marty saw what she'd bought for him.

As Terry stuffed the boxers into his pocket and started the car, Emily settled back beside Nicholas. A few minutes and they'd be home. She knew the route so well, she really didn't pay any attention until Terry drove right past Paddington Street.

"Terry, you missed the turn-off." She looked back over her shoulder.

Terry didn't answer. Instead, he turned the next corner and headed back toward the shopping center.

"Trouble?" Nicholas kept his attention fixed on Terry, a frown on his face.

"Take a look, Nick. The blue Ford. It's been following us since we left the Five Ways. I'll slow down. See if you can get a look at the driver."

A sense of unease settled in Emily's stomach. She'd forgotten all about the papyrus while she'd been caught up in her shopping. She twisted around in the seat to look out the back window. "We've got someone following us? Let me see."

"Don't make it so obvious," Nicholas snapped, the serious federal agent persona now firmly back in place. "Turn around toward the front and let me deal with it."

Terry slowed the vehicle a fraction more. "Can you see the driver?"

"All I can see is a man in what looks like an overcoat with a hat pulled down over his face."

"It's probably the man who was staring in the shop window. He was watching us as we left. He ducked into a doorway when he saw me staring at him."

"Why didn't you say something at the time?"

"Can you get the license plate?" Terry interrupted. "I'll radio it through to Control. They'll soon tell us who owns it. Of course, it could be stolen, but it gives us a place to start."

"Ah, Nicholas—"

"Not now, Emily. This is important."

"But, Nicholas, I—"

"Later. When we get home."

Emily shrugged. If they wouldn't listen to her, there was nothing she could do.

"Damn it," Nicholas muttered, "the license plate is covered in mud. I can get a partial. BLW... It ends with a seven, but the mud has obscured first two numbers. Maybe... No, that's all I can get."

Terry picked up the radio from the dashboard. "Control, this is Agent Banks. I want you to do a license check. I have a partial. BLW, miss the next two numbers and then a seven. It's a blue Ford Falcon Forte sedan. Probably a late 1999 model."

The radio crackled as the operator on the other end came back. Emily couldn't make out the words.

Terry depressed the switch and spoke again. "Yeah, yeah. I know how many blue Fords could start with those letters. Just see what you can do to narrow the field a bit. And make it a priority."

He placed the radio back on the dash and turned the car toward Paddington Street. "That's the best we can do for the moment. Now let's get this lady home."

Emily was the first out of the car when they reached the terrace house. Not waiting for the others, she walked up the front path to the door. Before she could knock, Marty opened it from the inside.

"I've bought you a present, Marty. Come into the living room and I'll show you." She grabbed him by the hand and tugged him after her.

Nicholas followed, grinning as he saw the big, tough federal agent, the top gun of the unit, trailing after her like a little lamb. He needed to discuss the tail they'd picked up with Marty, but he'd let Emily have her fun first. It was going to be interesting to see what she'd decided would suit Marty.

Emily tipped the shopping bag upside down on the couch. As the river of satin and laces settled, she flicked through the contents. Snagging up a burst of bright yellow, she handed it to Marty.

Nicholas chuckled. Another pair of boxers. These were satin. Quite innocuous...until Marty held them up. Both Nicholas and Terry took one look and started laughing. Nicholas laughed even harder when Emily took the boxer shorts and held them up to Marty's waist.

"There. Perfect. Your wife will love them."

The front of the boxers had a big black happy face printed on it. That wasn't so bad. It was the red floppy tongue hanging out of the mouth, falling down in the very front of the boxers that made him grin. As Emily wiggled the boxers, the tongue flopped up and down.

Nicholas tried to control himself and then gave up. Elizabeth Tomlins was not the type to appreciate another woman buying Marty underwear, let alone something like this. Marty would have to work fast to explain this one.

"Ah, thanks, Emily," Marty mumbled as he whipped the boxers away. "And *you* can stop laughing." He scowled at Nick. "Just wait until I tell them at the Agency what you've been up to."

"Actually, I've bought you a present, too, Nicholas," Emily piped up.

Oh-ohhh. After seeing what she'd bought for the others, he dreaded to think what she'd chosen for him. When she handed him a bundle of black fabric printed all over with deep red kiss marks, he thought she'd made a mistake. This was the outfit she'd bought for herself.

He held it up. Matching boxers. Was she trying to tell him something? He'd think on it later. Right now, he was just grateful she hadn't chosen something totally outrageous.

"Hey, how come you got a plain pair? You should have seen what she got for me," Terry said in an aside to Marty.

"Ahh, there's something special about these." Emily grinned. "Hold them up to your waist, Nicholas."

He did what she asked without thinking. A wary look crossed his face as she advanced on him in a sultry glide. An imp of pure devilment danced in her eyes and seemed to take control of her.

"Okay, I know I'm the wrong gender, but think of me when you're with your next lover. I'll give you a demonstration of how versatile these boxers are."

She walked the fingers of both hands up his chest and stroked the base of his neck with a feather-soft touch before creeping up further, skimming the outer edge of his ears. Then she tugged at his hair, pulling him down to drop light kisses along his jaw line. When she ran the tip of her tongue along his bottom lip, Nicholas had to struggle to swallow the groan threatening to break free.

Need slammed into him. Testosterone surged through his body, awakening parts of him he'd rather stayed asleep right now. Nerve endings jangled. The synapses in his brain fired in double-quick time, making him feel light-headed.

Bloody hell, if she doesn't stop this, I'm going to embarrass myself in front of my colleagues. What the fuck is she up to?

Emily wanted to deepen the kiss, but she had to remember this was a game. She couldn't believe how difficult it was. With a stern admonition to her libido to go back to sleep—*yeah right*—she continued her playacting, sliding her hands down Nicholas's torso to his hips. When he gave a half-stifled groan, she trailed one hand lower, flexing it on his denim-clad thigh before hooking both hands into the elastic waistband of the boxers.

Terry and Marty were laughing in the background, but she never once moved her gaze from Nicholas. She was too intrigued with the myriad expressions flashing across his face.

"Now, when your lover has you all hot and bothered," she whispered, her voice low and sexy, "all he has to do is this."

Stepping backward, she pulled hard. The Velcro fasteners at the sides of the boxers gave way and the garment parted, the front falling down. Nicholas's mouth dropped open in shock.

Emily couldn't help herself. She lost the sultry pose and burst out laughing at the expression on his face. "Easy access," she spluttered amid the laughter.

"Nice to see you weren't exempt," Marty retorted. "If I have to explain these to my wife, it's gratifying to see Emily took you for a ride as well."

"It's just a joke," Nicholas muttered.

With a grin, Emily gathered up her purchases. Before she left the room, she glanced back over her shoulder at Nicholas. "That's no joke. That's sex, my friend. Amazing what something like that will do for a relationship. I'm sure your next man friend will enjoy them." She left the room to the combined laughter of the other two agents.

When she reached the bedroom, she dumped the lingerie on the end of the bed and sat down. Damn, why did she do that? Somehow she needed to distance herself from the emotions curling about inside her. Teasing Nicholas was not the way to do it. It'd only make it harder when it came time for him to walk away.

She shook her head. Sitting up here brooding was not going to help the situation. She'd march downstairs and treat Nicholas like she did the other two agents. As newly acquired friends.

After all, what else could she do? He hadn't asked her to fall in love with him. This was her problem, not his. Pasting a happy smile on her face, she went back downstairs. The men were discussing the blue car tailing them home when she entered the living room.

"It's going to take time tracking down all Ford Falcon sedans with a number plate starting with those letters," Marty said. "But once we have a list, we can start eliminating those who don't fit. Are you sure it was a man and not a woman driving?"

"It certainly looked like a man." Nicholas ran a hand through his curls, grimacing as he did so.

"Okay, we eliminate all the little old ladies who drive blue Fords." Marty stood and paced across the room. "Did Control give you any indication how long it would take?"

Emily interrupted before Nicholas could reply. "I don't know why you're going to so much trouble."

Nicholas turned at her comment. "Emily, this is important. If we find out whose car it was, we very likely have the name of the person who tried to break in here to get the papyrus."

"I don't know why you're getting into such a tizz about it. It's easy."

"What's easy?" Nicholas scowled at her.

"Finding out where the car came from. You don't have to rely on computers."

All three agents looked at her, eyebrows raised.

Emily shrugged. "All you had to do was ask me, but you wouldn't let me speak."

"So who was driving the car?" Nicholas's voice had dropped down a tone, as if he were trying to control himself.

"Like I said, that's easy. Didn't you see the sticker low on the passenger side of the windscreen?"

"Emily?" Nicholas's tone was even more ominous.

"I don't know *who* was driving, but the sticker showed quite clearly the vehicle belonged to the University of Sydney fleet."

Chapter Eight

"You knew who it was and you didn't say anything?"

Emily rolled her eyes. "I have no idea *who* it was, but all the University of Sydney vehicles carry that sticker on their windscreen. I tried to tell you in the car, but all you were interested in doing was shutting me up. I figured you'd work it out for yourself."

Nicholas drew in a deep breath and let it out slowly. "You're right. I didn't listen to you. So now I will. Who has access to the vehicles?"

"Almost anyone on staff over a certain level. Certainly all the professors. And the administration staff. And the dean. And the—"

"Okay, I get the picture," Nicholas interrupted. "Next question. Do the vehicles have to be signed out?"

"They're supposed to be. The transport officer at Administration should have the details. Although I have to warn you, not everyone takes the time to play by the rules. Whoever it was may have taken the keys from the office without signing for them."

"Do you have the number handy? I'll give the office a ring."

Emily took a quick glance at her watch. "The number's by the phone, but it's after five. You may not get anyone now. The office closes at four."

"Worth a try," Nicholas muttered as he turned toward the phone.

Emily watched as he dialed the number, her mind going over the possibilities. Someone from the university had followed them today. Or rather, had followed her. The same someone who'd been staring in at her as she shopped for lingerie.

The idea gave her the creeps, more so because this meant it was someone she knew from the university. And that someone wanted the papyrus. Why else would anyone try to break into her house? She had numerous valuable antiques in the house, but her instincts told her that wasn't what they were after. It had to be the papyrus.

But why? Because it was valuable in its own right? Or because of what was written on it? Whatever it was, she needed to finish deciphering the hieroglyphics and get the papyrus out of her home. Regardless of the fact that completing the translation would catapult Nicholas out of her life.

"No answer, just a recording." Nicholas dropped the receiver back on the cradle. "Marty, can you and Terry drive over to the university and track down the dean? See if he can help us."

"No problem, Nick. Do you want us back here after that?"

"Yeah, I think so. I'd like you two to watch the front of the house tonight. I've got the back covered with the sensor lights. I'm sorry you're going to have to pull an all-nighter."

"Yeah, I'll bet." Marty grinned. "You owe me one."

After the two agents left, Emily turned to Nicholas. "If you can get the papyrus for me, I'll go up and work on it. The sooner it's done, the better."

"How long do you think it'll take?"

"Hopefully only a few more hours. With a bit of luck, I may be able to finish it tonight." She waited while Nicholas retrieved the papyrus and then headed out of the room, stopping at the entrance. "How about you try out some more of your culinary skills while I work?"

"What do you fancy?"

"Anything will be better than my usual burnt offerings," she laughed, as she left him to it.

ꙮ

Emily slipped the papyrus, along with her translation notes, back into the protective plastic sleeve. It wasn't finished, but it was close. Unfortunately, she'd run up against some symbols she hadn't seen before. She'd have to do some further research before she could complete it.

From what she'd already translated, if this ancient recipe actually worked, the Department of Defense had a powerful and valuable weapon. No wonder someone wanted to steal it.

She slid her hand up under her hair and massaged the back of her neck. She was stiff from bending over the desk for so long, the muscles aching every time she moved her head. A slight noise at the door of the office alerted her to the fact that she wasn't alone. A shiver trembled down her spine. It seemed as if the very air had become highly charged with crackling electricity. The fine hair on her arms stood up and a sweat broke out on her brow.

Never had she been so conscious of a man, or any other human being for that matter. Her body responded the moment he walked into the room.

"All done?"

"Almost." It was amazing how much of a struggle it was to get the word out. It felt like her brain had atrophied. Damn, she was acting like an idiot.

Before she could come up with anything else, Nicholas slid his hands under the fall of her hair and took over massaging her neck. The breath whooshed from her chest at his touch. She allowed her head to droop forward as he worked the stiff muscles. It was a mixture of pain and pleasure as his fingers dug in, loosening the knots.

As the stiffness ebbed away, the pleasure took precedence, infusing her mind with a sensual awareness that threatened to deprive her of the remaining air in her lungs.

She moaned as his hands fanned out over her shoulders under the edge of her tee shirt, skimming back to the column of her throat. His long fingers curled round her neck. Brushing lightly. Sensitizing the flesh. Igniting every nerve ending with little points of fire that danced across her skin.

His hands slid up her throat again, thumbs pressing in at the base of her skull. When he caressed the underside of her chin, Emily couldn't help herself. She tilted her head back to rest on his midsection, her gaze caught as the dark glitter of his eyes drew her in and held her captive.

"You're very good at this," she muttered. Her voice was husky and mirrored the intense sexual longing charging through her blood. Her thought processes grew cloudy, muddled by good old sexual tension. "I'll have to repay the favor some time very soon."

The mere act of speaking seemed to shatter the mood. It was as if a shutter slammed down over Nicholas's face, obliterating the gleam in his eyes. His jaw clenched and his oh-so-sexy mouth pulled into a tight line.

He dropped his hands and immediately stepped back, saying nothing for the moment. Emily lowered her gaze to the desk in front of her. Her hands fisted in her lap so tight she could feel the nails cutting into her palms.

She couldn't have said a word to save herself. A wave of disappointment, mixed with a hefty dose of feminine frustration, washed over her. In its wake, it left such a depth of longing Emily thought she would surely drown in it.

"Ahh...um, dinner's ready and it's getting late. You want me to lock that away?" He nodded to the papyrus.

Nicholas's voice was as husky as hers had been. Emily silently defied anyone to tell her he wasn't as affected by that massage session as she was. No matter what he claimed to be, she *had* got under his skin.

Problem was, she couldn't do anything about it. She wasn't going to be the one responsible for screwing up his psyche, confusing him about his sexual orientation. He was only reacting to her presence because she'd set out to change him. Well, no more. She couldn't do that to him. He was too nice a man. He deserved better than that.

"Yep, you can lock it away. I've done as much as I can tonight on the actual translation. I need to do some research and track down a couple of unusual symbols before I can go on."

Out of the corner of her eye, she watched him skirt around the desk to check she'd locked the balcony door. Without getting too close, he reached over and picked up the plastic envelope containing the papyrus. As he turned to leave the office, she said, "Will dinner wait for five minutes? I'd like to have a shower and freshen up."

"No problem," he muttered.

Then he was gone and Emily was left alone to agonize over all the what ifs and if onlys crowding her mind.

"Enough, Emily," she berated herself. "Go have your shower before you drive yourself crazy."

ꕥ

Nicholas closed the safe, moved the planter back and quickly returned to the kitchen. He tried to keep the thoughts bombarding his brain at bay with deliberate action. He opened the oven and used a mitt to lift the lasagna out, placing it in the center of the table. Then he added a bowl of tossed salad.

Now the wine. Grab the corkscrew—twist—turn—listen to the satisfying pop as the cork left the bottle. Fill the two crystal glasses standing in front of each place setting. All perfectly mundane tasks designed to drive the erotic images from his mind.

Concentrate on the food, Nicholas. Christ, he was turning into a house-husband. He'd done nothing *but* concentrate on food since meeting Emily. It seemed to have become the entire focus of his day. Well, that and the good professor.

He gathered up the dishes he'd used to prepare dinner and placed them in the sink, rinsing them in the hot water in preparation for stacking them in the dishwasher. Turning off the tap, he braced his hands on the edge of the sink and hung his head.

Damn, it wasn't working. All he could think about was the feel of Emily's soft skin under his hands. The look in her eyes as she'd rested her head on his stomach. Her intoxicating perfume teasing his senses. And the fact that he'd wanted to do so much more than massage her neck.

"You're an idiot, Nicholas Farley," he grumbled. "What the hell did you do it for? Now you've just made it harder on yourself."

And it wasn't the only thing that was hard. His cock tightened even as he struggled to clear his mind of the teasing, erotic image of the two of them rolling around on the four-poster bed upstairs. He turned the tap on and held his hands under the water in a vain effort to wipe away the feel of her.

"Are you okay, Nicholas?"

He spun around at the question. Some agent he was. He'd been so caught up in his thoughts he hadn't even heard her approach.

She stood in the doorway to the kitchen, her freshly brushed hair hanging about her shoulders, her face scrubbed clean. For once, she wasn't a clash of colors. She'd chosen a simple slip dress in a golden topaz shade that matched her eyes and made them seem more exotic. Tiny shoestring straps snaked over her shoulders and tied in tantalizing bows just begging for his touch.

He wanted this woman. Physically. Sexually. He wanted her like he'd never wanted any other woman. But it was more than that. He needed her. Like he needed to breathe. Not just for a week. Not even for a month. He needed her—for the rest of his life.

His eyes widened and his mouth dropped open in shock. Mr. Bachelor, *love-'em-and-leave-'em* Farley. He'd finally gone and done it. He'd found a woman he actually wanted to spend the rest of his life with. The man who didn't believe in love, let alone love at first sight, and he could well be on the way to falling in love with a kooky professor who couldn't even dress herself properly most of the time.

His father had met and married his mother all within the space of a month. He'd said he knew the moment he'd met her she was important to his future happiness. Guess he was more like his old man than he thought.

Hell, how about that?

"Nicholas, are you okay? You've got the strangest look on your face."

Emily moved further into the kitchen. What on earth was wrong with him? He looked as if he'd been beaten over the head with a very large lump of wood.

His mouth snapped shut and a fatuous grin spread across his face. "I'm fine. In fact, I'm great. Now come and eat this meal before it gets cold."

Emily slipped into the chair he held for her and waited while Nicholas served her. She had to say one thing for him—he was a good cook. His future partner certainly wouldn't starve. Just a shame it wasn't going to be her.

Oh, for crying out loud, Emily, quit it.

Wishing wasn't going to make it happen. The sooner she got that through her thick head, the better for her peace of mind.

She picked up the knife and fork and dug into the steaming lasagna. As she swallowed the first mouthful, she caught Nicholas watching her.

"Good?" He raised his eyebrows as he waited for her response.

"Hmm, lovely. You can come and cook for me anytime." *Stupid, Emily.*

She lowered her head and concentrated on her meal. Maybe she could keep her hormones in check if she didn't look at him.

For a while, the only sound was the scrape of cutlery as they both focused on their food. Emily was afraid if she spoke, she'd beg him to love her, both physically and emotionally. She couldn't do that to poor Nicholas. She wouldn't confuse him any further.

She finished her meal in silence. A silence fraught with tension. Her skin prickled every time she felt him looking at her. The mere brush of his hand against hers as they both reached for the salad bowl had her heart racing and her temperature rising.

Finally, she pushed her plate away. "That was terrific."

"Glad you liked it." Nicholas poured the last of the wine into his glass after silently offering it to her. "How long do you think it'll take you to finish the papyrus?"

"I'm almost there. I need to get in touch with a fellow Egyptologist at the University of Melbourne, but it'll have to wait until office hours tomorrow."

"Ah...Emily, you know you can't talk about the papyrus, don't you? This is a top-secret project now the federal government and the Department of Defense are involved."

"I don't need you to tell me that, Nicholas. I'm living it. Why else would I have my own personal bodyguard?"

"So why do you need to discuss it with someone else?"

"I need help translating a couple of hieroglyphs I've never seen before. I'll email him a drawing of the symbols and see what he comes up with. At best, we'll probably both be guessing if no-one else has ever seen these particular symbols before. Don't worry. I won't tell him anything about the papyrus."

"You reckon you'll be finished tomorrow?" He got up to remove the used dishes.

Emily found her gaze drawn to the long line of his back and the play of well-developed muscles in his upper arms as he rinsed and stacked the plates. Her mouth went dry and her heart beat fast with longing. Longing for something she couldn't have. Now or ever—certainly not with Nicholas.

"Emily?"

"Ah...yeah, right...tomorrow. I'll be finished tomorrow and you can call your buddies at the Defense Department to come get it."

She backed away from the table, looking for an escape, not only from Nicholas's magnetic presence, but also from her own troubling thoughts. "Look, I know I shouldn't land you with the dirty dishes, but I'm feeling pretty shattered. All this heavy concentrating on the papyrus. Do you mind if I cut out and leave the cleaning up to you? I thought I might climb into bed with a few text books on Ancient Egypt and get a head start on the research."

"Don't worry about the dishes. I'll take care of them. You go on up," Nicholas said as he dried his hands. "Are you sure you're all right?"

"I'm fine, just tired." She hovered in the doorway to the kitchen for a moment. "Well, if it's okay with you?"

She didn't wait for his reply. She bolted. Up the staircase and into the bedroom. Grabbing a robe and the first sleepwear that came to hand, she locked herself in the bathroom.

ജ ഏ

Nicholas called the cat in and locked the back door. Ria was fussing about being shut inside, but she'd just have to deal with it for a few more nights. At least until they caught whoever was trying to break into Emily's home.

Marty's visit with the dean of the university hadn't elicited much in the way of information. Whoever had followed them hadn't signed the car out. Still, Nicholas had his suspicions. He'd just have to wait and see.

Palming the radio Marty had left for him, he thumbed the switch. "You there, Marty?"

"Right here, Nick."

"Okay, we're all locked up in here and I'm about to go up to bed. If you see any action out front, give me a buzz on the radio."

"Hey, man, it's only just gone ten."

Nicholas waited, knowing Marty wouldn't be able to resist getting in a dig at him.

"Wahoo! Hear that, Terry? Nicholas baby is going to bed early...with the gorgeous Emily. Just remember, Nick, old buddy, you're supposed to be on duty. No sleeping on the job. But then you won't be sleeping, will you?"

"Get a life, Marty," Nicholas snapped before flicking off the radio.

With the cat at his heels, he ascended the staircase, pausing as the third tread from the top creaked in protest. There'd been no noise at all from upstairs for some time. He didn't want to wake Emily if she'd already dropped off to sleep. The light was on in the bedroom so maybe she was still reading.

He halted on the threshold, his breath ripped away by the vision that met his eyes. Emily had pulled the covers back and lay stretched out on her side on the creamy satin sheet, sound asleep. Her face in repose was still mobile—a frown pleating her brow before clearing, a small smile tilting her lips in an upward curve. She'd obviously fallen asleep while reading, the heavy textbook open beside her.

It was what she was wearing that held him rigid—the sexy black number with the red kiss marks she'd bought today. The little band of lace on the edge of the panties rested high on her hip, emphasizing the length of her legs.

The top, what there was of it, barely covered her breasts. The enticing little black bow nestled between her breasts cried out to be undone. He curled his hands into fists and resisted the impulse.

"Get with the program, Nick," he whispered. "You can't stand here all night. Just pretend she's not there."

Yeah right, he thought as he crept over to the bed. He pulled the holster and gun from the back waistband of his jeans. Removing the gun, he slipped it under his pillow, dropping the holster on the bedside table. His back-up weapon, the little .32 caliber Smith & Wesson that fit snug against his ankle, he placed in the top drawer. Reaching out, he gently lifted Emily's research books and placed them on the floor under the edge the bed.

Eyes averted, he shucked his clothes until he was down to his satin boxers. He was tempted to swap the navy blue boxers he was wearing for the pair Emily had given him. The ones that matched the almost non-existent outfit she wore.

No, too much of a temptation. *Go to bed, you damned idiot*, he silently cautioned himself.

He clicked on the bedside lamp and strode across the room to turn off the overhead light. As he moved back to the bed, Emily stirred and rolled onto her back. Bathed in the glow of the lamplight, she was an even more alluring picture, enough to drive his blood pressure up and set his heart to racing.

Resting his knee on the side of the bed, he started to reach down for the covers. Suddenly, he froze. Paralyzed. Caught in mid-action. Unable to move forward or backward.

All he could do was gaze down at the woman beside him.

"Where's your famous control now?" he asked himself in a whisper.

One side of her little top—the same top that was held together only by an itty bitty bow—had flipped back when she'd moved, exposing most of one breast. He felt like a voyeur, but he couldn't help himself, he had to look his fill.

His cock hardened, pushing at the front of his boxers. His heart pounded in his chest. Tremors rocketed through him as he fought to control the rampant lust raging through his blood.

"*Holy fuck*!" His tone sounded reverent, even to his own ears. She was like an Egyptian goddess. Hopefully, *his* Egyptian goddess—once he got this case out of the way.

"Nicholas?"

Emily's voice was husky with sleep...and something else. Something much more elemental. Or maybe that was only wishful thinking.

He dragged his gaze to her face. Her eyes were half-open, staring up at him. A knowing smile curved her lips. The tip of her tongue slid across her lower lip, the dampness glistening in the lamplight. He had a sudden desire to lower his head and capture the taste of her with his own mouth.

"Ah, Nicholas... I was dreaming about you."

"Probably a nightmare," he muttered, starting to draw back. He couldn't believe he'd been caught staring like this. He felt like a fledgling virgin. Juvenile. Embarrassed. Uncertain of himself. But so damn hot. On fire for Emily. Oh crap, was he in trouble!

Emily snaked her arms up and around his neck to prevent him moving. This was like an extension of her dream, with Nicholas gazing down at her with such longing mirrored in his eyes. "No, don't go yet. I want to tell you about my dream." Hell, she'd even take a good old-fashioned bout of lust right now.

"Um...I don't think this is such a good idea. Why don't you go to sleep and I'll do the same?"

She knew it wasn't a good idea, but with the papyrus almost finished, this may well be the last day with Nicholas. The final night. He would leave the moment she'd finished the translation. After all, there'd be nothing to hold him here then. Surely the powers that be wouldn't condemn her for one little kiss? Something to remember?

"Why don't you kiss me goodnight? Then I'll go back to sleep."

Nicholas groaned. "This is definitely not a good idea. I'm supposed to be protecting you, not ravaging you. This is an assignment, Emily. And the agent's manual tells me I'm not supposed to get involved."

Disappointment shafted through Emily...until she saw him lower his gaze to her chest. She glanced down to see one breast uncovered, the nipple already hard and throbbing. She knew she was being manipulative, but damn it, she needed this and she wasn't above using what God had handed out to her. She dragged in a deep breath so her breast lifted, the distended nipple clearly visible.

"Just one itty bitty kiss?"

"One kiss, Emily. One kiss and you go to sleep like a good girl."

"I have to tell you, Nicholas, I'm not a child."

"God help me, I know that," he muttered as he lowered his head and captured her mouth.

Emily sighed as she felt the soft glide of his lips, but it wasn't enough. She didn't want a tame goodnight kiss. She wanted the heat, the pounding heart, racing pulses. She wanted it all. *She wanted him.*

Good intentions flew out the window as she opened to him, all her previous self-imposed resolutions lost in the flood of desire coursing through her blood. When he would have ended the kiss and pulled back, she tightened her arms about his neck and drew him closer.

Fully cognizant of what she was doing, she drew him into the kiss, tempting him with the thrust of her tongue, allowing her actions to speak for her. She needed this night, this memory, to hold firm to when he left her.

She knew what she was doing was wrong. Both for her *and* Nicholas. But she wanted this night. Just one night. That's all she was asking for.

A memory to keep her warm when Nicholas was no longer part of her life.

Chapter Nine

Emily groaned in disappointment as Nicholas broke off the kiss and pulled back far enough to focus on her face. He stared down at her, an almost feral look in his eyes. Without being told, she knew his hunger was as great as hers.

"Emily, do you know what you're doing?"

"Do you want me?"

"Damn it, you know I do. If you have any doubts..."

His voice trailed off and he allowed his body to answer for him. He settled his weight half over her and pressed his hips close. Emily was gloriously aware of his state of arousal as he ground his hard erection against her.

"One night. That's all I'm asking for."

"We shouldn't do this. For a lot of reasons. First, you're a client. My assignment. I shouldn't get involved. On any level."

Emily's hand trembled as she traced the outline of his lower lip. Her breath escaped on a gasp when he touched the tip of his tongue to the pad of her finger before going on.

"Second, you'll probably regret this in the morning."

"I'll regret it more if I don't."

"And third, I'm a—"

"Third," Emily interrupted, "you're gay, or think you are. But I know you want me, so maybe you're not really certain where your interests lie."

"Damn it, I'm not—"

"Shhh! No more talking." She placed her hand over his mouth. "Just this one night, Nicholas."

Not giving him time to respond, she pulled his head down and fastened her lips over his, angling her head to gain greater access to the warmth and taste of him.

She knew the exact moment Nicholas gave in. He suddenly took control, his tongue thrusting, dueling with hers. She met his every move, drowning in a sea of emotion. She was gasping when he finally lifted his head, the breath snatched away by the depth of carnal hunger sweeping through her.

Nicholas slid his mouth down the line of her throat, leaving a string of butterfly kisses in his wake. She arched her back and sighed in delight as he nipped at her collarbone before laving it with his tongue.

He pushed the slender straps of her top off her shoulders in a light caress then trailed his finger along the lace trim hugging her breasts. Sensation surged through Emily. Her breathing grew ragged. Nipples peaked and pushed against the filmy fabric. She wanted to beg him to touch them, take the aching peaks into his mouth, but he had his own agenda in mind. As he fingered the trailing ends of the tiny black bow between her breasts, the tempo of her heart accelerated and tension curled in her gut.

"When you stepped out of that fitting room in this, I thought all my birthdays had come at once." He clutched one end of the ribbon and started to pull. "I wanted to grab hold of this bow and rip it open."

"So what are you waiting for? Be my guest." Emily held her breath as he undid the bow, one careful inch at a time. It was more erotic than having him rip it off her, drawing out the suspense, raising the anticipation level another notch. Her clit was already throbbing, her panties wet.

"If you set out to tease me today, you did a good job. I don't think I've ever been so uncomfortable." He chuckled. "Or so turned on."

"Actually, it wasn't deliberate," she said on a gasp as he slid his finger down between her breasts and separated the two sides of her top. "I was just trying to treat you like one of my girlfriends. I wasn't trying to be sexy or anything."

"Emily, you don't need to try. You just are," he said as he stripped the little black and red top from her body.

He lowered his head and ran his tongue over the fullness of one breast. She lost the ability to think, let alone talk. A moan escaped when he settled his lips over the pebble-hard crest, drawing the nipple deep into the warmth of his mouth. His hand lifted the weight of her other breast, rolling the turgid peak between his thumb and finger.

Emily threaded her hands through his dark hair and held him close. Her body arched like a bow, affording him greater access as he suckled deeply at her breast. The fire in her blood became a raging inferno. Each tug of his lips raised an answering spark deep inside her pussy, setting up a subtle ache that demanded fulfillment.

The pleasure was so great it was almost pain. Her heart pounded. The blood raced through her veins. The breath rasped in her throat as the feelings inside twisted tighter and tighter. She was almost at the point of screaming in frustration when Nicholas raised his head and covered her mouth with his, his tongue sliding across her teeth to thrust inside as he drove the tension higher still.

When he slid his hand down her body, feather-soft across the curve of her stomach, she moaned, the needy sound captured by his mouth. Her body temperature skyrocketed. Emily felt as if she were about to combust.

He trailed his fingers lightly across the satin fabric of her panties. Emily broke the kiss, her head angled back as she tried to drag much needed air into her lungs. *Oh God, don't let him stop.*

Then he cupped her, the heat of his hand like a brand through the material. She cried out and lifted her hips, pushing against him, trying to create friction where she most needed it. Creamy moisture flooded her pussy and her clit ached with an insistent throb.

"There's something I wanted to do the moment I saw this little number," he growled.

His husky voice, filled with desire, made her shiver in reaction. She gasped as he moved down her body and placed a kiss on her satin-covered hip.

She had to clear her throat before she could speak. "What was that?"

"I wanted to kiss each and every one of these pouty red lips." He proceeded to put his words into action.

Emily raised herself up on her elbows and watched Nicholas place his mouth over the first of the bright red kiss marks printed on her panties before moving on to the next. The sight was so erotic, the feelings inside her almost spiraled out of control.

The breath caught in her throat as he worked his way across the line of her panties, kissing the little red spots, continually moving down. She obligingly spread her legs as he traced the printed kisses with his hungry mouth. Her hips bucked in reaction. The fabric of her panties dampened even more with each ardent press of his lips until she felt his warm breath through the damp satin. She writhed on the bed, no longer able to keep still.

“Enough, Nicholas. I can’t take any more.” She arched her body to catch the next kiss, her action at odds with her words.

“Not nearly enough,” he murmured in a husky voice as he rolled her over onto her stomach. “I still need to kiss all the lips on this side.”

Emily groaned as he started at her side and moved across her ass, his breath hot against the satin. She ground her hips into the bed, trying to relieve the unrelenting pressure in her pussy.

When he appeared finished with his feast, she sighed with both relief and disappointment, only to gasp aloud when he slid her panties over her bottom and dropped a fleeting kiss on her bare skin.

“Lift up,” he whispered and as she did so, he disposed of her last item of clothing

He rolled her onto her back, curling up beside her, his mouth immediately fastening on her engorged nipple and his hand sliding over her stomach. When he sifted his hand through the curls at the juncture of her thighs, she raised her hips, seeking more. Needing more. Unable to control the movement of her body.

Without being told, he knew what she craved. He trailed his fingers down over the swollen folds of her labia. She gasped. Sensation slammed into her, her heart pounding so hard it was a wonder she didn’t pass out. She couldn’t remember ever being this responsive, this willing to give of herself with any man before. Surely this couldn’t be wrong?

The ability to think disappeared when he parted her and pressed his thumb over her aching clit. He ran the tip of his finger along the length of her then slipped one finger into her throbbing pussy. Emily bit her lip to keep from crying out. She arched her hips, wanting him to go so much further.

"God, you are so wet and hot," he whispered.

When he inserted a second finger and thrust deep, Emily did cry out. He withdrew and thrust again establishing a rhythm designed to drive her crazy.

Tension gripped her, like a spring wound too tight. She pumped her hips in time with his thrusts. It wasn't enough. She wanted more. God help her, she wasn't going to be able to hold it together much longer. The orgasm build deep inside her. She felt like she was going to snap, but she didn't want to be alone when she reached the heights. She wanted Nicholas there with her.

"Now, Nicholas," she gasped out. "I need you now."

She moaned long and low as he withdrew his hand. He lifted his weight over her and made a place for himself between her legs. The satin stroke of his rigid cock high on her inner thigh had her panting for more. Then he nudged at the entrance to her pussy.

"Wait." Shit, she'd almost forgotten. Protection.

"Emily, I can't wait much longer," he groaned, his voice husky.

More by feel than sight, Emily reached out and snagged the edge of the dish of condoms. Hand shaking, she lifted it high over the bed, and lowered it down toward Nicholas. "Quick. Choose."

Her hand slipped. The dish tilted, the contents raining down. Colorful foil packets fell around them like so much confetti, sticking to their sweat-slicked bodies, sliding over them to pool on the bed around them.

Emily's lips twitched. A chuckle bubbled up. Nicholas dropped his head to rest on her breast and started to laugh. The humor of the situation relieved the tension somewhat, but it was still there, simmering just beneath the surface. It needed only the stroke of his hand or the soft touch of his lips to drive it high again.

Nicholas lifted his head and grinned. "I only need one."

"Oh, yeah?" Emily plucked a little foil packet from its resting place on his shoulder. She peered at the label. "Glow in the dark. This will do for the moment."

He held out his hand for the condom, but Emily shook her head. "How about you let me do the honors?"

"Be my guest." Nicholas grinned and, taking the bowl from her, reached across and placed it on the bedside table. Then he rolled onto his back and tucked his hands behind his head. He was all for letting the woman help out in issues like this.

Emily came up on her knees and handed him the foil packet. "Hold that for a minute."

"Hey, you'll..."

His voice trailed off when Emily leaned over and curled her fingers around the width of his rigid erection. The blood pumped into the organ, making his cock throb in her hand. His balls tightened with the need for release. When she lowered her head and probed at the slit with the tip of her tongue, the breath snagged in his chest.

Heat shot through him, as if the blood in his veins had caught fire. When she whipped her tongue around the engorged head, he groaned. And when she opened her mouth and took him inside, he thought he'd expire on the spot.

Without any direct order from his brain, his hips lifted off the bed, driving his cock into Emily's hot mouth. She slid her lips back to the top, teeth gently scraping his rigid length. He shivered with reaction, sweat breaking out on his forehead as he tried to hang onto his self-control.

Holding his cock at the base with one hand, she cupped his balls with the other and applied a subtle pressure. A guttural cry tore from his throat. His hips pumped, driving him forward and Emily took every inch of him.

She had her back to him and bent over as she was, he had a perfect view of her delectable ass. His hand trembled as he ran his fingers down one curved cheek. She tightened the muscles in her ass and wiggled her hips as if in invitation.

He moved his hand down between her thighs, sliding a finger into her creamy dampness. Emily moaned around his cock, her hot breath searing the sensitive nerves. When he thrust again into her wet pussy, she increased the speed and depth of her movement, taking him deep and sliding back to the head, only to swallow him again.

Nicholas's breathing fractured. God help him, he wasn't far from coming. His balls tightened and pulled up close to his body. Much more and he'd lose it. The scent of sex filled the room, a powerful aphrodisiac.

Sliding his finger from Emily's pussy, he slid his hand up between the cheeks of her ass. Her own cream made the movement slick. He circled the ring of her ass then pressed against the tight muscle. Emily dragged her mouth from his cock and gasped, pushing backward against his hand.

"God, Nicholas, I can't wait any longer." She turned toward him and held out a shaky hand. "Quick, where's the condom."

His own hand shook as much as hers as he handed over the packet. She tore it open and extracted the rubber sheath.

Then she rolled it down over his hard cock. Nicholas took the initiative and flipped her onto her back, coming down over her. She pulled him in and positioned him at the entrance to her core, raising her hips to him.

Emily watched him, the tension taking hold again. The saliva dried in her mouth. Sexual hunger such as she'd never known flooded her system. She kept her gaze fixed on his as he slowly slid home. Filling her. Stretching her. Making her whimper with need.

She tightened her internal muscles about him, dragging him deeper, afraid he'd pull back at the last moment. He started to move, hips controlling the depth of his strokes. Emily wanted to scream in frustration.

"Damn it, Nicholas. Don't tease," she groaned. "I want you hard and fast. Fuck me. *Now!*"

As if her words had broken the restraints on his self-control, he propelled himself forward. He withdrew and slammed home again. She raised her hips, meeting his every thrust. The only sound in the room was the rasp of their labored breathing. The slap of sweat-slicked bodies meeting in a torrent of sexual-fueled ardor.

Emily gave in to the feelings swirling within her, riding with him to unimagined heights. Heat raced through her blood until she felt like she was on fire. Her skin was so sensitized each brush of his hand was like a brand, on her flesh and on her soul.

She felt the ripples begin deep inside of her. The spasms spread, gathered force, driving out every other thought but this moment in time. With one final thrust, Nicholas pushed her over the edge into a world that existed only for lovers.

Heat.

Soaring emotions.

Molten-hot feelings.

Sunburst stars and flaring skyrockets.

And Nicholas was there with her, crying out his own release, holding her close and sheltering her until they slowly drifted back to earth. Until reality took over again and Emily found herself back in her own bedroom.

"Wow," she murmured when she could catch her breath.

"Tell me about it!"

When Nicholas rolled to his side, pushing aside the little foil packets littering the bed, Emily went with him. She curled up close and rested her head on his shoulder, her hand gliding across his chest. Never had anything felt so right, this being here with Nicholas. But what was he feeling? Did he regret it?

"Nicholas, I—"

"Shhh. Go to sleep, Emily."

"But—"

"Shhh."

Tomorrow. Yes, I'll deal with it tomorrow. She closed her eyes and allowed sleep to claim her, taking with her the memory of Nicholas's exquisite lovemaking.

ꙮ

Emily opened her eyes and stretched, arms raised high above her head. Her body ached pleasantly and her brain quickly reminded her why. She turned her head on the pillow, expecting to see Nicholas lying beside her. The bed was empty, the only indication she hadn't slept alone the indentation on the pillow beside her. Rolling over, she stared at the alarm clock, hardly able to believe what the little red numbers were telling her.

"Good gracious, it's almost eleven o'clock."

She flung back the sheet, slid her legs over the side of the bed and sat up. Tiny foil packets clung to her naked skin. She couldn't prevent a satisfied smile creeping across her face as she plucked the condoms from her body. She was a believer in safe sex, but this was ridiculous.

The smile still firmly in place, she grabbed a robe and fresh underwear and shut herself in the bathroom. As she showered, her thoughts turned to the previous night. She'd been wrong. One night was not enough. She wanted a lifetime with Nicholas. A lifetime of love. But what did Nicholas want?

Suddenly she was impatient to find out. She turned off the shower and quickly toweled off before slipping on her bra and panties. With the robe clutched about her shoulders, she returned to the bedroom and donned a skirt and blouse.

She didn't have her glasses with her to color coordinate her outfit, but who cared what she looked like? She needed to find Nicholas. That was the most important thing.

Not bothering with shoes, she hurried downstairs to find him sitting in the living room going over what looked like a mountain of computer printouts. She abstractedly noticed he'd washed the curls she'd created from his hair. Now it lay dark and sleek against his head. It really did suit him much better this way. Gave him a sexy, dangerous edge that did wonders for her libido.

She crept up behind the couch and leaned over to drop a quick kiss on the top of his head, only to have him pull sharply away. "Good morning, Nicholas." She frowned at his reaction. "Why didn't you wake me?"

Nicholas jumped up and moved away from the couch. "You needed your sleep." He flicked a quick glance at his watch. "It's almost lunchtime, but I can make you some toast or a sandwich if you're hungry."

"No, I can wait. Nicholas, about last night—"

"I'm sorry about last night. It should never have happened." He moved further away from her. "Don't you have some work to do? We need to get that papyrus out of here today." He gestured to the heap of papers lying on the couch. "And I have a lot of work to get through."

She watched in silence as he retrieved the papyrus and translation papers from the safe. Her heart almost broke as she observed the careful way he handed them to her so he didn't have to touch her. Then he stepped back. Away from the couch. Away from her.

Emily bit her lip to stop herself giving in to the temptation to say anything else. She wasn't going to beg him to spend time with her. After all, she'd only asked for one night and it looked like that was all she was going to get.

"So shouldn't you get on with it? How long will it take you to find out what those symbols mean? The ones you've never come across before?"

"If I can get hold of my friend, it shouldn't take too long." She kept her eyes averted so he wouldn't see the pain she was suddenly sure was reflected there.

"Okay, I'll call someone from the Australian Defense Intelligence Organization to come and pick the papyrus up this afternoon."

Emily had to get out of there before she broke down and cried. She turned her back and walked out of the room without saying a word. Taking the stairs two at a time, she entered her office and flopped down into the chair behind the desk, allowing the papyrus to fall unheeded onto the desktop.

She felt bereft. Plunged into a depth of misery she would never have believed existed. Tears slowly trickled down her face. What had she done?

It didn't matter that she'd told herself just one night to remember. Deep in her heart, she'd expected Nicholas to be as swept away by their lovemaking as she'd been. She'd prayed last night was a beginning, not an end.

The easy camaraderie that had developed between them had disappeared, swept away by one night of passion. It was obvious he was trying to pretend it hadn't happened. He didn't *want* to remember. And it was her own fault.

Guilt hit her in crashing waves. She wiped at her face with the back of her hands as the tears tumbled down faster. Yes, it *was* her fault. She'd known Nicholas was gay. He'd told her. Well, Marty had, and Nicholas hadn't refuted the statement. She'd deliberately set out to try to change him. Because she hadn't believed he was truly gay.

How many women had tried to reform a recalcitrant man only to have it blow up in their face? She'd tried the impossible. She'd wanted to turn a gay man straight. Show him what he was missing. And look where it had landed her.

A tiny voice in the back of her mind reminded her of the intense lovemaking of last night. How could he make love like that to a woman if he were gay? Maybe he was bi? It didn't really matter now anyway. She'd been the one to instigate what had happened. She'd tempted Nicholas beyond endurance. If the man was already confused about his sexuality, how much more so would he be now? How could she have done that to him? It was totally selfish of her. She hadn't set out to hurt him, but it was obvious by his reaction that she had. He'd made it perfectly clear he didn't want to be reminded about last night.

Guilt at her actions clawed at her as she wiped her face before pulling the papyrus from the protective sleeve. The best thing she could do was get the translation finished so Nicholas could leave. She wouldn't be responsible for hurting him more than she already had. He was too nice a man to have his head screwed up by a color-blind, crazy professor.

Taking up a pen, Emily copied out the symbols she needed translated and scanned them into the computer. Quickly typing out a message, she attached the symbols and emailed them to her academic friend in Melbourne. While she waited for his reply, she made a clear copy of the translation. All she had to do now was fill in the blanks when she had the answers.

Then Nicholas could leave. Walk out of her life forever. And hopefully put his own life back on track—without her interference.

Chapter Ten

Nicholas paced from one end of Emily's little living room to the other. His work lay forgotten on the couch. It'd only been an excuse anyway. Something to keep his mind off the woman upstairs.

Damn it, how could he have been such a fool? He'd broken the most sacred rule in the agents' handbook.

Don't get involved with your client.

He'd done more than that. He'd gone and fallen for the woman who was the subject of his assignment.

Way to go, Farley!

To make matters worse, he'd made love to her.

And if that wasn't bad enough, he'd made love to her while allowing her to go on thinking he was gay. Or at least confused as to which side of the fence he belonged on.

He should have told her. He silently reminded himself that he *had* tried. But he should have tried harder, made her listen. He shook his head. This wasn't Emily's fault. He shouldn't have touched her at all. At least, not until the case was over.

For crying out loud, he'd never wanted to fall in love. He hadn't gone looking for it. It was his normal practice to cut and run the moment a woman looked like getting serious.

Until Emily.

Now he wanted it all. The slippers by the fireside. The little woman waiting at home for him. Tiny replicas of him and Emily running to greet him when he came home from work.

He grimaced at his chauvinistic thoughts. What he really wanted was permanence. Emily by his side for the rest of his days. To love and to cherish. To grow old together.

Guilt filled him at the hurt he'd caused her. And he *had* hurt her. He'd seen it in her eyes before she'd turned away.

He wanted to go to her and convince her he really did care, that he didn't want this to end, but he couldn't. Not yet. He'd broken enough rules as it was. He would just have to wait. He couldn't afford to mishandle this. It was too important to him.

ꙮ

Emily laid her pen on the desk and glanced at her watch. It was well after lunchtime. No wonder her stomach was grumbling. She'd been up here for hours. She frowned. Strange Nicholas hadn't called her for lunch. Was he that angry with her? Chagrin overrode the hunger as she thought again about what she'd done to him. No wonder the poor love didn't want to spend time with her, even to eat lunch.

At least the translation was complete, her friend having emailed her with the meaning of the obscure symbols. Now Nicholas could leave. She blinked back the tears that immediately filled her eyes.

"Enough, Emily," she muttered. "This is all your fault. Now it's time to put it right. Let him go." Gathering up the papyrus, she tucked it and the translation into the plastic bag. Next, she collected all her working notes. With both clutched in her hands, she left the office and started down the stairs, only to halt in shock at the sight that met her eyes.

The front door was open wide and the hot summer sun beamed in, creating an oasis of light in the darkened hallway. Standing right in the patch of sunlight was Nicholas, his arms around the shoulders of a much younger man. A young man who had his own arms around Nicholas and his head resting on his shoulder.

"Don't worry, it'll be okay. We'll make it okay. Everyone will accept it, you'll see."

A crack as wide as a chasm fractured through Emily's heart as she heard Nicholas's words.

"Yeah, I can just imagine how they'll react when I turn up with a boyfriend," the younger man snapped out.

"They love you, Toby. Don't worry, I'll talk to them. Now get out of here before my client comes down."

That's all I am, Emily thought as she watched the man leave and Nicholas close the front door. *I'm nothing but an assignment. An experiment Nicholas tried and decided he didn't like.*

The crack in her heart widened.

Now she didn't need to wonder if Nicholas were truly gay. The evidence was right there in front of her eyes. Only an idiot would disregard it. She might be a little crazy at times, but she was no dummy. She wanted to cry for what might have been, but she couldn't allow herself the luxury.

Not now.

Not ever.

An errant thought flitted through her mind. She didn't think she'd ever get over loving Nicholas. And she suddenly realized she did love him. This wasn't just lust. Or the need to prove a point. It went much deeper than that. She had a feeling there would never be another man like him. Dear God, she'd have to face that for the rest of her life.

This was nothing like the tepid emotions she'd had for Maxwell. In comparison, what she'd felt for Maxwell D'Lacey had been comfortable warmth, like a favorite shoe, well-worn and molded to the wearer's foot. Maxwell had fitted himself around *her* lifestyle, changed himself to fill the gap in her life created by a loneliness she hadn't even been aware of.

Okay, so he'd taken advantage of her. Made a fool of her with other women. Lied and deceived her. But she knew now what she'd felt for him had never been the grand passion. Although it had hurt at the time, her heart had eventually recovered.

What she felt for Nicholas was different. Nicholas was fire, clawing at her insides, burning fiercely in her heart. Her feelings for him colored her every thought, filled her every moment, both waking and sleeping. It was something she knew would be with her until the day she died. Because that was the only way she would ever forget Nicholas.

Bullshit, nothing but melodrama, Emily, shouted a little voice in her mind. "Oh shut up," she whispered. "I'm leading with my heart here, not my head."

Gathering her courage about her like a second skin, Emily plastered a bright smile on her face and clattered down the stairs. When she reached the hallway, she handed the papyrus over to Nicholas.

"All done. You can call your army friends now. All my notes are there as well. No doubt they'll have to be destroyed."

"Actually, I've already called the Defense Department. They're waiting for me to contact them to tell them it's finished. It'll only take them ten minutes to get here. They have someone standing by."

“Well, while you do that, I’m going to get some washing on.”

She turned and walked away. When she entered the kitchen, she leaned against the cupboard, biting her lip to control the tears that threatened to overflow. Pushing aside the ball of misery lodged deep inside her, she entered the little laundry set off to one side of the back door. Maybe some good old-fashioned housework would take her mind off it all.

Grabbing the laundry basket, she lifted it up and slammed it down on the table beside the washer. After separating out the whites, she loaded the rest into the machine and added washing powder. Nicholas came in just as she closed the lid. She kept her eyes on the control panel as he stepped up close behind her, but she had no hope of ignoring his presence.

His heat reached out to her, driving her own body temperature higher. The breath caught in her chest and her heart beat out a welcoming refrain. Shame Nicholas wasn’t listening.

“Okay, Captain Robertson and one of his minions will be here shortly to pick up the papyrus. As soon as they leave, I have to go out. Something important I have to deal with. Marty will come by and stay with you until I get back.”

That did make her look up, a perplexed frown on her face. “Why do I need a babysitter if the papyrus is no longer in the house?”

“Whoever is after it won’t know you’ve finished the translation. Plus there’s one other thing you haven’t thought of. The info is stored in your head, making you a prime candidate for a kidnap. You’re still at risk. *And* the Department wants to catch this person. So I’m afraid you’re stuck with me until we get him.”

Before Emily could say anything, a knock sounded on the front door. As Nicholas went to answer it, she turned his words over in her mind. Oh, the bittersweet irony of it. Nicholas wasn't leaving. At least not yet. She would still have him with her. At the same time, he was separated from her by a gulf wider than she was physically or emotionally capable of bridging.

The low murmur of men's voices came from the hallway, but she had no desire to join them. The defense guys had what they wanted. A translation of the papyrus. They no longer needed her input and neither did Nicholas.

All of a sudden, it was difficult to swallow, as if a lump was stuck in the back of her throat. Breath catching, she started to cough. Quickly turning on the laundry tap, she held her hand under the flow and drank deeply. Once she had herself under control, she wiped her mouth with the back of her hand, eyes watering as a result of the coughing—and maybe something more. But at least she had a good excuse for the dampness of her eyes when Nicholas again entered the room.

"You okay?" He patted her on the back before guiding her out to the kitchen.

"Yeah," she croaked. "Breathing the laundry powder made me cough, but it's fine now."

"Hey, look who I found on the doorstep when I ushered those army types out." Nicholas stood aside and gestured to the man who stood behind him.

"Hi, Marty, it's good to see you. Although I'm not certain I still need a bodyguard."

"Miss Emily, I'll guard your body any time you like." Marty wiggled his eyebrows and twirled an imaginary moustache.

Emily couldn't help herself. She burst out laughing. Right now, she needed a bit of light-hearted comic relief and Marty was very good at it.

"Why, thank you, sir," Emily replied in her best Southern belle voice.

"If you're finished with the frivolity," Nicholas interrupted coolly, "I have to go." He turned to Emily. "I'll be back before dinner. Don't worry about cooking. I'll bring some Chinese back with me."

She watched him leave the kitchen and listened to the sound of his footsteps on the polished floor of the hallway. The decisive click as the front door closed behind him.

"I swear, that boy acts more like a husband than I do," Marty chimed in. "I don't know what you've done to him, Miss Emily, but all I've heard the last few days is what food he wants brought in, what's he's cooking you for dinner. He seems totally fixated on food."

Emily ignored Marty's words. She was too busy wondering whether Nicholas *would* come back. Maybe he'd had enough of her and would just pass the case onto Marty. Then she rejected the idea, knowing Nicholas would keep his word. He'd be back in time for dinner. And bed!

That gave her something else to worry about.

Bed—and Nicholas sharing that bed with her.

Chapter Eleven

Emily lay curled up on the couch watching television with Marty. As the intro for the seven o'clock news flicked onto the screen, she cast a glance at her watch to verify the time.

It was getting late. Where was Nicholas? Maybe he'd decided not to come back after all. She wouldn't blame him if he had. Not after she'd done her best to screw up his life by trying to initiate him into the pleasures of loving a woman when he so obviously leaned in the opposite direction.

She pulled her legs up and dropped her head to rest on her bent knees. Who would have guessed how her life would change with the advent of another birthday? She cursed the day the Egyptian urn, with its hidden treasure, had arrived.

Now she had a black hole where her heart should be and a crazy cat that spent all her time hovering over the shards of broken pottery. Maybe Ria knew something she didn't. The darn cat had certainly been acting strange since the urn had come into the house. Perhaps the urn was cursed.

Yes, that'd be right. Just my luck.

Maybe there *was* a curse. She certainly felt as if there was a blight over her life, especially her love life. First, with his oh-so-perfect looks, was Maxwell, who'd lied through his teeth to her and set out to deceive and betray her. It had taken a long time to get over that little fiasco.

Now there was Nicholas. Perfect for her in every way...except one. Oh, he hadn't set out to deceive or to hurt her—she'd managed to do that all on her own—but the result was the same.

Heartache, such as she'd never experienced before. Black despair eating at her soul. And this time she had a feeling she was never going to get over it. More than just a feeling, a conviction.

Nicholas had ruined her for any other man. No one else would ever come close to him, or the feelings she had for him. She'd never believed in love at first sight before, but holy crap, it sure felt like that's what it was. How could she possibly fall in love so quickly? And there wasn't a darn thing she could do about it, beyond hiding it deep in her heart and praying she'd find a way to learn to live with it.

When a knock sounded on the front door and cut across the depressing thoughts, Emily jumped. This time she didn't rush to open it. Instead, she allowed Marty to do the honors. Somehow, she knew it was Nicholas.

"I'd about given up on you," Marty said as he opened the door to admit Nicholas. "Thought you'd decided to make a night of it. I was just trying to work out how I'd tell my wife I'd be sharing a bed with the delectable Miss Emily."

"She'd skin you alive," Nicholas retaliated as he entered the living room. "No problems here?"

"Of course not. Emily and I have had a great afternoon playing games. She's a whiz at checkers. You'll have to play with her some time."

Emily closed her eyes briefly. Oh, she'd like to play with Nicholas, but checkers weren't on the agenda. She had more adult games in mind.

Nicholas glanced across at her and held up the plastic carry bag. “Hungry? I came prepared to satisfy your appetite.”

If only, Emily silently wished. And it wasn’t food she was thinking of. She uncurled her legs and stood up. “I’ll just get some plates and napkins. Marty, are you staying for dinner?”

“No, I’d best get home. The wife is holding dinner for me.” He turned to Nicholas. “Terry and I are on call tonight, so if anything happens, you can get me on the radio.”

“Well, let’s hope it does so we can find out who’s behind all this,” Nicholas replied. “I’ll be glad to get this job over and done with and get on with my life.”

A wave of sadness swept over Emily. He couldn’t wait to get away from her. With the assignment finished, he was free to leave, to wipe all memory of her from his mind. She felt like crying. She left the room and entered the kitchen, determined to keep it together until he’d gone.

When she returned with plates and forks, and a bundle of paper napkins, Marty had gone. Nicholas had unpacked the containers of food and placed them on the coffee table. He gave her a swift grin. “Seems I’ve done nothing but hassle over food the last few days. Never realized how much of a preoccupation it can become.”

“Don’t you know food, with the right person, can be as erotic as the raunchiest toolbox of sex tools?” Emily quipped before she could help herself.

Nicholas stilled and turned his gaze on her. Emily felt the heat from the tip of her toes clear up to her face. She shivered. *Great. Why did I open my big mouth? I don’t need to remind him I’m the wrong person.*

Focusing on the food again, Nicholas took off the plastic lids. The spicy aroma of the beef in black bean sauce and sweet and sour pork teased her taste buds, making her salivate.

Damn, she'd forgotten to have lunch earlier. Seeing Nicholas with his...friend had wiped away any thought of eating.

Well, misery certainly hasn't affected my appetite, she thought as she served herself a small helping of fried rice before adding an equal quantity of the beef dish.

"Is that all you're having? Aren't you going to try the pork?" With a frown, Nicholas handed her a set of chopsticks.

"I'll come back for seconds when I've finished this lot."

Nicholas lowered himself onto the floor on the other side of the coffee table, his long legs curled under him. He quickly served himself and started on his meal.

Emily watched as he scooped food onto the chopsticks without any effort at all. When she tried to imitate him, all she managed was two grains of rice. The second attempt resulted in pretty much the same. She looked up to find Nicholas watching her, a grin on his face.

"You'll starve at that rate. Hang on."

He laid down his chopsticks and moved around to sit beside her on the couch. Emily could smell the tang of his aftershave when he leaned close, his arm about her shoulder as he reached for her hand.

"Place the bottom one like this so it doesn't move. Then use the top one to hold the food."

He moved her hand down toward the plate and manipulated the chopsticks to grasp a piece of beef. When he raised her hand to her mouth, Emily automatically opened to capture the sliver of succulent meat.

She swallowed. "That's all very well and good, but what about the rice? A piece of meat is easy compared to those slippery little grains." Her voice was husky as she tried to concentrate on the food, rather than the man beside her.

“It’s only a matter of practice.” He guided her hand back to the plate, scooped up some of the rice and aimed it toward her mouth. “Now you try it.”

Emily breathed a sigh of relief when Nicholas moved around to his side of the table again. She couldn’t deal with his closeness. She wasn’t equipped to handle the rush of feelings that assaulted her.

Determined to keep focused on her meal, she tried to wield the chopsticks as Nicholas had shown her. After half a dozen abortive attempts, she dropped them onto the table and picked up a fork. She attempted a smile as Nicholas laughed. “If I don’t want to be here all night, I’d be better off using this.” She waved the fork before digging in.

When they were finished, Emily carried the dirty dishes into the kitchen. She’d deal with them tomorrow. Right now, she was too tired to care whether the dishes ended up clean or not. She needed to be on her own, to lick her wounds in private. It didn’t matter the wounds were invisible. They were no less real.

She stuck her head around the living room door. “I’ve got some work to do upstairs. I have to start preparing some new lesson plans for next semester. So if you don’t mind me deserting you, I think I’ll get to it.”

She didn’t wait for his reply. She fled, taking her heartache with her.

Once upstairs, she decided to have a shower first. She didn’t need to start on the new lecture schedules yet. It was just an excuse to keep busy—and away from Nicholas.

Opening the drawer in the bedroom, she reached for a teddy and then hesitated. The mood wasn’t right for sexy satin and lace. She searched through the colorful layers of erotic lingerie until she found a plain cotton nightgown. A neck-to-knee job, without a single frill. The sort of thing her mother would wear. In fact, come to think of it, her mother had given it to her for her birthday last year.

ꟿ

Nicholas yawned and glanced at his watch. Shit, he hadn't realized how late it was. He'd been staring at the television screen for hours without taking it in. He grimaced. Watching television had only been a ploy to give Emily enough time to go to bed before him.

Hopefully, she'd already be asleep and he could slide in beside her without waking her. He didn't think he could keep his hands off her if she was waiting for him wearing one of those abbreviated numbers she called a nightie.

He made certain the cat was inside and the doors and windows all locked. With a last check to make certain the security lights at the back of the house were on, he flicked off the rest of the lights and dragged himself upstairs. On tiptoes, he entered the bedroom only to stop short.

The bed was empty, the cover still drawn up over the pillows, the lamp beside the bed burning brightly. But no Emily. Where the hell was she?

He did an about turn and quietly made his way to the office. The soft glow of the lamp highlighted the desk and there sat Emily, head pillowed on her arms. She was sound asleep. Her dark hair had partially escaped from its clip and wisped around the side of her face.

She was dressed in a pale pink cotton nightie with little rosebuds scattered across it. For a moment, he just stood, taking in the scene. A part of him was disappointed she wasn't wearing the black and red outfit from the night before, or something similar. Then he looked at her again and admitted to himself that in some way, this was even more erotic.

She looked sweet, virginal, but at the same time alluring. Because *he* knew the fire hidden beneath that innocent exterior. He'd burned with it last night and if everything went according to plan, he would wallow in the sensuality of that delectable body for the rest of his life.

His cock hardened and he had to struggle to rein in his rising libido. If he wanted any sleep tonight, he'd better get his hormones under control.

Leaving Emily for the moment, he went back to the bedroom and turned down the covers on the bed. When he returned to the office, he gently lifted her into his arms. She murmured his name in her sleep, but didn't wake. Instead, she snuggled close, her arm sliding up around his neck.

He stood holding her, assaulted by a wave of love for this woman. The warmth of her body released the evocative scent of flowers. It seemed to curl about him, invading his senses, lodging deep in his heart. From this moment on, whenever he saw a flower, it would always remind him of Emily.

With a stern word to his body to behave, he carried her into the bedroom and slid her into bed, dragging the cover up over her shoulder. She immediately turned on her side and buried her head in the pillow. He waited a moment, but she didn't stir.

Crossing to his side of the bed, he followed his nightly ritual. First, the Glock under his pillow. Then he slid his back-up weapon into the top drawer of the bedside table. As he closed the drawer, the bowl of foil-covered condoms that once more resided on the table caught his attention.

He never had asked her why she kept a bowl of condoms beside her bed. He shook his head at the futility of giving into thoughts about the number of ways he could use up those little packets. Now was not the time.

Within seconds, he'd stripped to his boxer shorts. He had a sudden desire to change into the pair Emily had bought for him. Not stopping to analyze his reasons, he grabbed them out of the bag lying under the bed and quickly stepped into them. With the satin cool against his skin, he slid into bed beside her. Now all he had to do was pretend she wasn't lying there with him and he might be able to get some sleep. *Yeah right!*

ജ്ജ

Nicholas heard the growling in his sleep. It seemed to radiate out from his chest until it vibrated through him and filled his mind with a low-pitched humming. It quickly became an intrusion, one that couldn't be ignored. He struggled up through the layers of cotton wool that seemed to have filled his brain and fought for consciousness.

When he was reasonably sure he was actually awake, he could still hear the growls, still feel the vibration on his chest. He cracked open his eyes and looked down to find Ria sitting on top of him. Shit, the darn animal wanted to go out.

"Damn it, Ria. Why couldn't you go when you were out in the garden?" He glared at the cat, only to have the stubborn feline nip at his chest. "Ouch. Bloody hell, cat, I'm coming. You don't have to bite me."

He dislodged Ria from her perch, sat up and swung his legs over the side of the bed. Still groggy, he watched the cat streak out of the room as he struggled to stand.

That's when he saw it. The light beaming into the bedroom from the outside sensor lights.

Someone was in the back yard.

He shook his head to clear the last vestiges of sleep from his mind and reached under his pillow to retrieve the Glock. His hand fit around the butt of the gun as if the manufacturer had fashioned the weapon expressly for him. It was like an old friend, an extension of his arm.

Taking care not to wake Emily, he tiptoed out of the room and down the stairs, avoiding the third top tread. One step at a time, he crept into the kitchen and over to the back door. He'd almost made it when his bare foot came down on something sharp. Several somethings.

He bit his lip to prevent himself crying out in reaction as the object cut into the underside of his foot. Kneeling down, he felt around in the dark until his hand encountered a sharp piece of broken pottery.

For fuck's sake, couldn't the bloody cat at least keep them out of the walkway?

What was it about this pot that had the cat so stirred up? He'd watched her drag the pieces out one at a time into the garden. By the feel of it, she'd hauled the rest of the urn down here tonight in preparation for tomorrow's removal excursion.

With the last shard brushed aside, he stood up, dragging in a sharp breath as he put his weight on the throbbing cut on the ball of his right foot. He drew on his training, ignored the pain and unlocked the door. A high-pitched creak echoed through the kitchen as ho opened it. Damn, he'd meant to oil the door hinges, but he'd forgotten.

He eased the door a little wider and waited while the cat streaked outside before stepping out and to the side. Weapon extended and supported by both hands, he dropped down on one knee and traced a visual path across the garden.

Unless someone was lurking behind one of the flowering bushes, the yard was empty, the intruder long gone. Still, it wouldn't hurt to search the area, in particular the overgrown patch near the back gate that the fingers of light barely reached. After all, that's what he was here for.

Senses alert, gun at the ready, Nicholas crept through the garden toward the back fence. Ria stalked at his side, keeping pace with him. When they were almost at the bushes, he paused and waited for his eyes to adjust to the decrease in light. The cat forged ahead, turning to face him, the fur on her back raised as she emitted a low feral growl.

What now? Was someone hiding in the bushes and Ria was trying to tell him?

Crouched low, he moved forward and reached out to part the shrubs, only to have Ria swipe at his hand with her paw, her claws digging in and leaving a trail of blood.

"Damn it, Ria, what the hell is wrong with you?" he whispered.

The cat backed up until she stood beside a scratched-over pile of dirt. Partially buried among the soil was a broken piece of pottery. He shook his head in disbelief. This was obviously the repository for the broken urn and the cat was guarding it as if she were afraid he'd desecrate it.

He couldn't believe it. Held up by a cat. If the guys at Control heard about it, he'd never live it down.

ꙮ

Emily stirred in her sleep, rolled over and flung her arm out. Her subconscious tried to drag her back into the warm and comfy layers of the dreamscape. She resisted, pushing back the world she'd created inside her mind and struggling for reality.

She slowly opened her heavy eyelids only to have them flutter closed. Her body fought to disobey her, but she persisted. She forced open her eyes again and her brain clicked into gear.

Something wasn't right.

A frown pulled at her forehead. She always left the lace curtains on the balcony doors open. She liked to see the moonlight filtering through, creating patterns on the polished timber floor.

If she woke during the night, she liked the fact that the room was never pitch black. Not that she was afraid of the dark, but she was a big enough klutz during the daylight hours. How much more so would she be in a fully darkened room?

But something was definitely wrong. This wasn't the ethereal glow of the moonlight. The room was much lighter, bathed in the harsh light beaming in through the glass doors. It pushed back the darkness, illuminating far more of the room than moonlight would.

She'd pulled herself up into a sitting position before her brain registered that the light was coming from outside. Something else suddenly hit her. Nicholas wasn't in the bed beside her.

Was someone in the backyard?

Sliding out of bed, she crept over to the doors, gently easing one open and stepping outside. Grasping the wrought iron of the balcony rail, she peered over, searching the garden for Nicholas.

When she spotted him down on his hands and knees talking to the cat, she breathed a sigh of relief. It was okay.

Obviously, Ria had wanted to go and had made certain Nicholas knew. Smart cat.

Emily smothered a yawn as she re-entered the bedroom. A glance at the clock told her it wasn't even five o'clock. She'd go back to bed and get on with her dream.

She had just set one knee on the bed when she heard it. A slight scraping noise as if someone had dragged a piece of furniture over her polished floor. She frowned. Had she imagined it?

No. There it was again. *And* it was definitely coming from inside the house.

The sensor lights were still on. Therefore, Nicholas was still in the garden with Ria.

So who was in the house?

Snatching up the robe lying over the end of the bed, she shrugged into it, not bothering to tie the long trailing belt. On bare feet, she crept over to the bedroom door and stepped out onto the upstairs landing. She paused, held perfectly still, and listened.

She heard the furtive sound again. There was someone in the living room. *The papyrus!* They were after the ancient manuscript and they didn't know it was no longer in the house. If she called out to Nicholas, it would alert the intruder. She'd have to deal with it herself.

Fear overwhelmed Emily for a moment. It made her heart pound and her hands tremble. Her legs suddenly felt like jelly. Then the anger cut in and swept aside the fear. How dare this person invade her personal space, come uninvited into her home?

She was tired of this whole damn thing. If it wasn't for that bloody papyrus, she wouldn't be in the mess she was in now. She wanted her nice quiet life back and she couldn't even have that until the would-be thief was caught and Nicholas had gone. To hell with it, this was going to end right now.

Breath held, she crept back into the bedroom and over to the bedside table. Sliding open the top drawer, she lifted out Nicholas's back-up weapon. For a moment, she almost dropped it. She'd never handled a gun in her life, but she'd seen plenty of movies.

How difficult could it be? It wasn't as if she'd have to fire it. No sane person would take on someone who held a gun pointed at him. She'd be perfectly safe. She grimaced, hoping her lopsided reasoning was sound.

Pulling the little gun from its diminutive holster, she held it up to the light. She assumed it was loaded. There'd be no point in having it for protection if it wasn't.

Sooo...every gun has a safety catch, right, Emily? Hell if she knew. The movies said so. All she had to do was find it. She didn't think it would actually be necessary to use the weapon, but it was better to be safe than sorry.

She turned the gun over, inspecting it from all angles. Maybe that little lever thingy on the side. That had to be it. She flicked it with her thumb, gratified when she saw it move. She just prayed it *was* the safety.

The gun held tight in her right hand, she started downstairs, almost tripping headlong down the staircase as she stepped over the third top tread. Righting herself, she held tight to the banister and kept her weight balanced on the extreme outer edge of each step.

When she reached the bottom, she found the front door wide open. She frowned. Surely Nicholas had locked it before going to bed? She shook her head. No way would he be so careless.

Heart thumping, she edged into the living room, stepping out of the doorway. The room was black, the heavy drapes drawn tight against the night. She waited for her eyesight to adjust to the darkness, listening for any sign of movement. She even held her breath so the sound of her breathing wouldn't be audible.

The room was deadly quiet. For a moment, she thought she must have imagined it. That it had all been part of a dream. Then she heard the faint scratching in the corner of the room. The slithering sound of something being moved. A whispered curse, bitten off before it gained resonance in the darkened atmosphere.

Damn it, she was right. Someone *was* there. Fear took hold again. Her heart raced in her chest. The blood pounded through her veins and beads of cold sweat broke out on her forehead. Palms slippery, she tightened her grip on the gun, pointed the barrel at the corner of the room where the sounds had come from and stepped forward.

"Don't move a muscle or I'll plug you full of holes." Emily was pleased with herself. There, that sounded tough, just like the good guy in all those Westerns she loved to watch.

There was an instantaneous reaction from the intruder. A shadow, slightly darker than the rest, rose up from the floor, detached itself from its surrounds and stepped toward her. Immediately, a renewed rush of fear hit her at the intruder's movement. She held the weapon tighter, her finger curled around the trigger.

"I said don't move. I have a gun here. I'll shoot." She deepened her voice, striving to make it sound more menacing. Of course, she knew she wouldn't shoot. She didn't want to be responsible for shooting *anyone*, even a sneak thief who came uninvited into her house under the cover of darkness.

When the intruder moved again, Emily stepped back another pace. The dangling end of her tie belt was her undoing. She stepped on the strip of fabric, effectively halting any movement. She tried to kick the piece of material out of the way, but only succeeded in catching it about her ankle. It was like a living entity, twisting and curling, tying her in knots.

Balance gone, Emily felt herself falling. With her free hand, she reached out for the wall, but she was too far away. Gravity took over, pulling her down. As she hit the floor with a resounding thud, her finger tightened reflexively on the little trigger.

The weapon discharged, filling the room with a reverberating echo. A loud curse spiraled up from the corner of the room, followed by a heavy crash and the sound of shattering glass and clattering furniture. The rank smell of cordite filled her nostrils, fogging her brain for the moment.

When she'd recovered enough to sit up, the little gun was still clutched in her hand. There was no movement from the other side of the room. Horror swamped her and she dropped the weapon as if it were a hot potato.

"Mercy, I think I've killed someone."

Chapter Twelve

Nicholas glanced over the garden again. The yard was empty. The only felon around here was a crazy feline, but there was no doubt someone *had* been here.

Fear suddenly slammed into him and curled in his gut. Fuck, he'd left the back door open. Anyone could have crept into the house while he was fussing around with the stupid cat.

Adrenaline pumped through his blood as he sprinted to the door, the laceration in his foot protesting the abuse. He'd left Emily unprotected, innocently asleep in the wide double bed.

He'd almost reached the back door when he heard it. The sound of a weapon discharging from inside the house, echoing loudly in the silence of the night. *His* weapon. The little snub-nose he'd left hidden in the top drawer of the bedside table.

His heart thumped loudly as the implications hit him. Someone was inside the house and the woman he was pretty sure he loved more than life itself had needed to protect herself.

Emily.

A rush of adrenalin and an intense fear for Emily's safety gave Nicholas a speed he would never have been capable of in normal circumstances. He hit the back door running, skidded through the kitchen and raced down the hallway, his feet pounding on the timber floor.

In the blink of an eye, he registered the open front door. The Glock extended before him, he crouched, his ears tuned for the smallest sound. Where the hell was Emily?

"Ohmygosh, what am I going to do?"

The horrified whisper came from the living room and he had no difficulty recognizing the voice. He no longer needed to guess where Emily was.

He came out of his crouch and sidled up to the doorway. His immediate response was to rush into the darkened room to make certain Emily was okay. His training kicked in and he paused, assessing the situation before charging in.

His brain quickly processed an overview of the layout of the room, visualizing the placement of the furniture and mentally programming in the position of the main light switch. Easing the safety off the Glock, he stepped into the room, hitting the switch just inside the room to activate the overhead lights. In a semi-crouch, prepared for anything, he surveyed the room, mouth open at the scene that met his eyes.

Had he stepped one foot further into the room, he would have fallen over Emily. She sat on the floor at his feet, a stunned expression on her face as she blinked dark-fringed, topaz eyes in the bright light.

She'd obviously thrown a robe on over her little cotton nightie. At the moment, the robe was open, the trailing tie belt caught about her feet. His Smith & Wesson lay on the floor close to her right side. It didn't take a genius to work out what had happened.

"You okay, Emily?"

At her nod, he turned his attention to the only other occupant of the room. Their would-be thief lay sprawled on the floor, caught up in a mess of rich potting soil, broken planter pot and crushed fern fronds. Beside him, the panel of false flooring removed, yawned the open recess that normally hid the safe, a silent testament to his intentions.

Damn, more broken pottery pieces for Ria to bury. The undisciplined thought slipped into Nicholas's brain before he could prevent it. He mentally kicked himself and dragged his attention back to the matter at hand.

The identity of the intruder didn't surprise him. He'd suspected him almost from the beginning so it came as no big shock, but it would to Emily.

"I figured it was you, D'Lacey. Bit late to come calling, isn't it?"

He heard Emily's gasp even before he flicked a glance down at her. She was shaking her head in disbelief. A movement on the other side of the room had him swinging his gaze back to Maxwell. The man was now on all fours, scrabbling about in the spilled potting mix as he tried to stand. Right now, he didn't look so debonair. Nicholas was secretly glad. The jealousy he'd harbored at Maxwell's place in Emily's past frittered away.

"Take it nice and slow, my friend," he warned as he leveled his weapon at the man. "On your feet and take a seat on the couch. One wrong move and I'll use this." He kept his eyes, and his gun, trained on the man as Maxwell levered himself up and limped over to the couch.

"She could have killed me," Maxwell wailed as he tried to brush soil and bits of fern off the front of his trousers.

"She didn't, but I could, so mind you don't make any sudden moves."

Emily, from her position on the floor, heard the sound of Maxwell's voice, but still couldn't believe it. She had to see it with her own eyes. Pulling the satin strip out of the belt loops of her robe, she untangled it from her feet. Now was hardly a good time to remember it had always been too long. She'd meant to shorten it so she wouldn't trip over it. She shrugged fatalistically. Things like that were always happening to her so why should tonight be any different?

She reached out and gingerly picked up the little gun then pushed herself to her feet. Once upright, she looked over at the couch. It *was* Maxwell. But a Maxwell like she'd never seen before.

His hands and clothing were dirty, his hair mussed and his oh-so-perfect face had a scratch down one cheek. And if that wasn't bad enough, he was whining. Maxwell oozed charm to get his own way. He manipulated everyone in sight. He never whined.

"You could have shot me. How could you do this to me, Emily? Look at me." He extended his arms wide to encompass his disheveled exterior.

Emily saw red. How could she... She couldn't even complete the thought. How could *he* do this to *her*? Invade her privacy and the security of her home. Scare her half to death.

Anger swept through her and she started toward him. She waved the hand holding the little gun as she yelled, "What the hell are you doing in my home?"

Nicholas grabbed hold of her arm and pulled her to a stop. He reached over her shoulder and gently eased the gun from her hand. "I don't think you need that any more, sweetheart. The safety's still off. You could shoot him."

"I'd *like* to shoot him," she ground out through clenched teeth.

"I can understand that, but not right now." Nicholas grinned. "I want you to go up to the bedroom and get the radio off the bedside table. Bring it back down here to me. I have to contact Control to get a pick-up car sent out."

"But I want to hear what he has to say for himself."

"And you will, but first the radio. Please?"

Emily sighed with impatience, but did what Nicholas had asked. She turned the hall light on before she raced up the stairs to retrieve the radio. When she entered the living room again, she handed it over and held her tongue while Nicholas called for a car.

"Can we question him now?" she queried when he dropped the radio onto the lounge chair.

"Can't see why not. I'd like to know his reasons for wanting the papyrus too, although I have my suspicions."

She turned and looked at Maxwell. He huddled on the couch, his hands alternately brushing at his clothes and smoothing his hair. Suddenly, he seemed smaller. Less...well, she didn't really know. Just less Maxwell. Not the same self-assured man who'd bedeviled her at work. Who had taken her heart and trampled over it, used her *and* her money, and lied to her the whole time. Now he simply looked pathetic, his lips pursed in a pout like a sulky child. Emily's lips quirked in the beginnings of a grin. How the mighty have fallen.

But that still didn't excuse the invasion of her privacy.

"Why did you do this, Maxwell?"

"Good question, Emily." Nicholas focused on Maxwell. "How about a good answer, D'Lacey?" He moved up and stood shoulder to shoulder with Emily, presenting a united front.

Maxwell appeared to shrivel even further and Emily could fully understand why. Nicholas seemed to have changed in some subtle way. He'd become the true professional. The trained federal agent. He radiated authority. An aura of menace surrounded him, ruthlessness stamped on his features. He wanted answers and he was going to get them, and Maxwell seemed to know this without being told. He opened his mouth and started speaking, his voice coming out in a little boy whine.

"I needed the papyrus."

"Well, that's obvious," Emily snapped in a sarcastic tone of voice. "But we want to know why. I mean, you couldn't translate the hieroglyphics. You're not an expert in that field. So why?"

"I didn't care what it said. I just needed the papyrus itself."

"But why?"

Nicholas interrupted. "I can hazard a guess. You needed money. Right, D'Lacey?"

Maxwell nodded his head vigorously. "Yes, that's right. I needed money. I had a buyer, a private collector of antiquities, lined up. I could have made thousands from the sale of the papyrus. I didn't give a damn what was written on it."

"But Maxwell, I don't understand." Emily shook her head, a perplexed frown on her face. "You have a good salary. You drive a fancy sports car. You own a luxurious apartment in the best part of Sydney. You wear only designer clothes. Why on earth should you need money so badly you'd break into my house to steal the papyrus?"

"I needed to pay off some debts in a hurry," he whined.

"Speak up, D'Lacey. We didn't hear you." Nicholas towered over him, the Glock still held menacingly in front of him.

"It was a gambling debt. A private high stakes game. I lost and they were pressing me to pay. I didn't have the money. This was the only way I could think to make lots of money in a hurry."

Emily was so angry she almost couldn't get the words out. "You...you break into my house and try to steal the papyrus. You followed me. You scared me half to death tonight when I thought I'd killed you. *And it's all for a gambling debt?*"

Her voice rose as the anger took over. She struggled to control it. "It wasn't good enough you stole from me when we were together? It wasn't enough you abused my trust? Now you put me through this?"

"But, Emily, there wasn't any other way. The people I owe money to are dangerous. They won't wait any longer. You don't want to see me hurt."

"Oh, yeah? Don't bet on it." Emily stalked away from the couch, her steps eating up the distance to the other side of the room. When she ran out of space, she turned and strode back to Maxwell, hands clenched at her sides to prevent her reaching out and smacking him one.

"I always thought you were smart, but only a fool goes down this track. I can't believe you would do this to me. To yourself. Well, you're going to have to deal with the fallout now. This is a federal case. Your charm won't help you out now."

"Emily, you have to help me," Maxwell wailed. "You can't let them lock me away. Think of what we once meant to each other. Of what we had together."

"Why, you slimy creep. All I ever was to you was a convenience. An easy way to get money to support your gambling habit. I was just the poor, dumb sucker you used. It was bad enough you stole from me, but you also played around behind my back, using *my* money to pay for your other women. You did nothing but lie to me the whole time we were together. And you think I should help you now? You have got to be kidding. You're on your own this time."

"But, Emily—"

"And that brings me to another thing," she interrupted. "How the hell did you get in here tonight? I took your keys back off you when we broke up."

"Maybe with these. They were still in the lock of the front door."

Emily turned to find Marty and Terry standing just inside the room. A set of keys with a big yellow smiley face dangling from the key ring hung from Marty's raised hand.

"So that's where they ended up." Hands on hips, Emily turned again to Maxwell. "Still up to your old tricks, I see. You stole them when you came over the other night, didn't you?"

Nicholas jumped into the conversation. "If you had the keys to the front door, why did you come over the back fence?"

"Dean Williams let slip you were Em's bodyguard and not just a friend. It was the only way I could think of to get you out of the house. I knew you'd go and investigate if the security lights were activated. I thought I'd be able to creep around to the front and retrieve the papyrus while you were out the back. I didn't plan on Emily waking up and coming down to catch me. *Or* that she'd have a gun."

He looked so put out, Emily wanted to shake him. She glared down at him instead. "You're lucky I didn't blow a hole right through your lying little body, you...you...worm."

"You want us to take him in, Nick?" Marty marched over to stand behind the couch, his hand on Maxwell's shoulder.

"No, I've already called for a car. They should be here any minute."

Emily moved away from the couch. She couldn't stand to be near Maxwell, he disgusted her so much. She suddenly halted when she spotted the mess in the corner of the room. The safe concealed beneath the floorboards in plain view. The planter stand that normally stood over it lying on its side, one leg hanging on a drunken angle. But it was what was spread around the open safe that made her blood boil.

"You murdered Abigail!"

"What the hell's going on here?" a voice snapped from the doorway. "Control sent us out to pick up a break-and-enter, not a murderer."

Nicholas looked up to find two co-workers, weapons drawn, standing at the entrance to the living room. "You can put the gun away, Mackenzie. There's been no murder."

The two agents advanced into the room. "Then who the heck is Abigail?" a perplexed Mackenzie asked.

"Guys, meet Abigail." Nicholas waved a hand in Emily's direction, trying to control the twitching of his mouth.

Emily was down on her knees gathering the remains of the crushed fern into her arms. *And* talking all the while to the damaged plant.

"Oh, you poor thing. What has the bad man done to you?" She plucked the broken fronds away from the core of the plant. "Poor Abigail. It's going to take you ages to recover from the shock of this, isn't it, sweet thing?"

"What's with her? She crazy or something?"

Nicholas leveled a frown at Mackenzie. "There's nothing wrong with talking to plants. Lots of people do it." Damn it, *he* could call Emily crazy, but no one else was going to get away with it. He swung his gaze back to Emily as she continued crooning over the mangled leaves.

"It'll be all right, Abigail. You've got some new leaves coming through right here. And look, you've got a baby. Oh, Abigail, you've got a baby right down here at the bottom."

The plant cradled in her arms, Emily jumped to her feet and quickly moved over to the men. Nicholas hardly had time to react before she dumped the fern into his arms. The remains of the damp soil spilled from the roots and clung to his naked chest. He had to juggle his weapon to keep from dropping the plant.

"Look, Nicholas, she's got a baby. She'll recover, but it'll take a while before she's as big as she was before. Hold her while I get something to put her in for the night. She'll be in shock, poor love."

As Emily darted out of the room, Nicholas stood there like a fool, the remains of the Boston fern clutched to his chest. He shook his head. This was one assignment he would *never* live down.

Emily was back within minutes with an empty pot. She gathered up some of the loose soil on the floor, took the plant from him and transplanted it into its new home.

"That will do for the moment." She placed the pot in front of the fireplace and turned toward the agents standing around the couch. She glared at Maxwell. "She'd better not die, you creep."

Nicholas cleared his throat. "I think it's time we got this scumbag out of here, don't you? Take him in, Mackenzie. I'll do the paperwork when I get there."

Emily watched as they bundled Maxwell out of the room. The last she heard of her past lover was his whining as the agents closed the door to the house. She mentally dusted off her hands. Another chapter of her life closed.

She turned to Marty. "How come you and Terry are here? Did you hear Nicholas radio in?"

"Good question." Nicholas tried to wipe the damp soil off his chest, succeeding only in smearing it further.

"Couldn't sleep," Marty replied. "And when I can't sleep, I do what I do best—worry. I started to get concerned about you and Emily here on your own without any backup. Thought I'd do a drive-by and check everything was okay."

"Yeah, he rang me and woke me from a perfectly good sleep to come with him," Terry chipped in. "Dragged me out of a terrific dream. I was just about to get it on with—"

"Enough of your fantasies, Banks." Marty grinned. "Emily doesn't need to know how your sick mind works."

"Whatever your reasons, I appreciate it. Although Emily had the situation well under control." Nicholas started to chuckle. "She nearly shot the guy with my Smith & Wesson, didn't you, sweetheart?" He turned to Emily, a frown on his face. "Which reminds me. Where did that round go?"

Emily spun about and looked at the corner where all the debris was. She had a vague memory of glass shattering when she'd hit the floor. Then she spotted the framed photograph on the wall over the fireplace.

"Oh, no, look what Maxwell did to my parents' photo."

"Ah, Emily, you did that yourself," Nicholas said. "That's obviously where the bullet landed."

He followed Emily over to the photograph. The glass was shattered, littering the floor beneath. "Look out for your bare feet on that glass. You'll cut yourself."

"I'm not worried about cutting myself. Look at my parents' photograph. It's got a hole in it." She reached up, ran her finger over the small hole and felt the spent bullet buried in the timber wall behind. "How am I going to fix that?"

Marty crowded in behind her to get a better view. "I wouldn't worry too much. It just looks like his belly button."

"He's got clothes on." She snorted in disgust. "How can his belly button show when he's got clothes on?"

Nicholas placed a comforting hand on her shoulder. "It's all right, Emily. Photography shops can do wonders these days. I'm sure they can fix it. Now come and sit down and I'll have Terry make us some coffee." He guided her over to the couch and pushed her down.

"But I should clear up this mess."

"Tomorrow's soon enough. We'll have the place shipshape in no time at all."

As she sat there and listened to Nicholas and Marty discuss the case, she realized what Nicholas had just said. *We.* He'd said *we.* Did that mean he'd still be here? The case was over. She'd thought he'd leave the moment it was finished. *But he said we.*

A rush of pleasure at his words filled Emily. As Terry returned with four cups of steaming coffee, she buried it at the back of her mind to savor later.

"So what's been going on here?" Terry said as he handed Nicholas one of the mugs. "I notice you're wearing Emily's present, Nick. Found them useful, did you?"

Nicholas glared. Terry grinned and moved on to Marty, offering up another cup of coffee.

Emily glanced at Nicholas and for the first time took notice of what he had on. The pull-apart boxers with the red kiss marks she'd bought him the day before. Shame she hadn't gotten to try out those Velcro fasteners. But if he were staying, maybe there'd still be an opportunity. Both to try out the boxers *and* to see if there was a chance for them as a couple.

Nicholas's cold silence seemed to have disappeared in the events that had taken place tonight. He'd been worried about her. *And* he'd called her sweetheart. Twice!

Some of the guilt she'd been carrying about over her plan to initiate Nicholas into the pleasures of loving a woman dissipated. Perhaps she really had convinced him he could find happiness with her. A mental picture of Nicholas hugging the young man in her hallway fluttered through her mind. Maybe he'd just been saying goodbye. Men sometimes hugged each other, if they were really close.

She dragged her thoughts back from the precipice they teetered on and listened to Terry and Marty teasing Nicholas.

"Well, at least you don't have to pretend any more," Terry quipped. "Boy, did the guys at the Agency laugh when they heard about that. They were just about falling down in the aisles."

Emily frowned. What was Terry talking about? And why was Nicholas frowning so hard when he'd been grinning only moments before? She watched as both Marty and Nicholas surreptitiously tried to shut Terry up, but he either didn't see their furtive movements, or chose to ignore them.

"Big macho Nicholas Farley. The heartthrob of the Agency. Having to act like he was gay. It's the best joke we've heard for a while." Terry burst out laughing, totally oblivious to the sudden tension in the room.

Emily leaned forward and gently placed her cup on the coffee table. She slowly uncurled her legs and stood. It felt as if her brain had shut down. As if her system had received a shock, far greater than any shock she might have suffered from having someone break into her house. More severe than the effects of firing a gun for the first time in her life. She wasn't even certain she'd heard correctly.

She advanced on Nicholas, vaguely conscious Marty had pulled Terry out of her path. When she stood directly in front of him, she gazed up into his face, searching for she didn't know what. Maybe something that would tell her this was all a joke and what she'd just heard Terry say was a lie.

What she saw was shame. And chagrin. A bright red flush of guilt that climbed up his features to color his whole face.

She stepped back a pace. Her hands grew clammy as she formulated her next question. Somehow, she knew her whole future hinged on his answer. “Are you telling me you’re *not* really gay?”

Chapter Thirteen

Emily held her breath. Each beat of her heart was hard and measured, with what seemed like an impossibly long pause in between. She felt as if she were standing outside of herself, watching from afar as the scene unfolded.

An out of body experience. The sort of thing people talked about after they'd died and been brought back to life. But how could that be? She wasn't dying. But then, maybe she was. Inside, where no one could see.

"Nicholas? Are you gay?"

Without saying a word, Nicholas shook his head.

"You're not gay?" Emily marveled that her voice came out so quiet and controlled when all she wanted to do was scream at him.

"I'm not gay, Emily. I'm a normal heterosexual male."

"*Why?* Why did you tell me you were gay?"

"I didn't. Marty did and I just went along with it."

"But why?"

Cracks began to appear in her calm façade. Emily wasn't certain how much longer she could keep it together. The hard, cold lump in the pit of her stomach started to uncoil, releasing anger into her system. She felt it building deep inside her.

"You didn't want a man in the house hitting on you," Terry interrupted. "That's why Marty told you he was gay. It was the only way we could think of to get you to accept a bodyguard living with you twenty-four hours a day."

Terry sniggered. "It was the greatest joke ever. Old Nick here having to pretend he was gay. His best undercover identity yet."

"Shut up, Terry," Nicholas ground out, all the while keeping his gaze firmly fixed on Emily. "Once the scenario was set, I had to go along with it. We needed an agent in the house to guard you and the papyrus."

"The means justifies the end. Even if it involved lying to me? Is that what you're telling me?" The anger gathered force, filling her with heat, tearing away the last of her self-imposed restraints. "You lied to me," she yelled. "You know how I feel about being lied to."

"I'm sorry."

"The three of you have been having a good laugh at my expense. Poor dumb Emily. Let her think the big macho bodyguard is gay. You made a fool out of me." With each word, her voice rose.

"Calm down, Emily."

"Calm down? *Calm down.* Don't you tell me to calm down. Have you any idea what you've put me through?"

"What I've put you through? How the hell do you think I felt every time you walked out in that sexy underwear?

Vaguely, in the background, Emily heard the sound of someone choking. *Probably Terry trying not to laugh at me,* she thought inconsequentially.

"I thought it wouldn't matter to you," she said. "You were supposed to be gay. And what about that young man you were hugging in the hallway this morning? Was that just part of the undercover story? So I'd continue to believe you were gay, even after last night?"

"That was my younger brother, Toby. He really *is* gay. He came to me because he wanted me to help him tell our parents. He wants to come out, but is worried how they'll take it."

"I changed my clothes in front of you. I slept in the same bed with you. Because I thought you were gay," she spat out, clenching her fist and thumping him on his bare chest.

From the corner of her eye, Emily caught Marty edging Terry toward the living room door. In the stress of the moment, she'd forgotten they had an audience. If this had to happen, she would have preferred it to be in private, but it was too late now.

"You think it was any easier for me, watching you walk around in next to nothing?" Nicholas glared at her. "I'm a normal, red-blooded male. How the hell do you think I felt? I wanted to tell you, but you were a client, my assignment. I had to wait until the case was resolved."

"That's all I was to you. A client. More than that, I was obviously the standing joke at the office. Poor dumb, stupid Emily. Can't even tell if a man is gay or not."

"Damn it to hell, don't talk about yourself like that." Nicholas ran his hand through his hair. "None of this was of my making. Okay, I should have told you before this, but I wanted to get the case out the way first. You were never the butt of anyone's teasing. I was. It was me they were laughing at."

"Yeah, right. The great stud of the office. Well, you can go back and tell them you added another notch to your bedpost."

"For crying out loud, stop being so melodramatic. It wasn't like that."

"You could have told me last night when we made love." A swamping surge of pain overrode Emily's need for privacy.

"When *I* made love. You were just satisfying a biological urge. But you still could have told me."

"I tried to tell you last night. You wouldn't let me talk."

"Well, obviously you didn't try hard enough. Do you realize the guilt I suffered today? I thought maybe we had a chance and then I come downstairs and you wouldn't talk about it. I knew you were regretting what had happened. I thought I'd screwed up your mind by tempting you into making love to me, a woman."

"Don't you think I had my own guilt to deal with? I'd broken every rule in the book by getting involved with a client. I *was* regretting it, but only because I was on a case. I *was* going to tell you. Damn it, I tried." Nicholas scowled. Fucking hell, why couldn't Terry have kept his mouth shut?

He'd wanted to tell Emily the truth. Had planned to spill the beans after everyone had left. He was going to tell her he loved her and ask her to marry him. Maybe not straight away, but he'd wanted to give her time to get used to the idea. This wasn't the way he wanted her to find out and it was clear he wasn't getting through to her. Why the hell couldn't she put aside her hurt feelings and listen to him?

A light flashed on in his brain. He hadn't actually told Emily he loved her. Maybe that was the only way to reach her and no time like the present. He suddenly wished the other two agents gone. He'd rather do this without an audience. Before he could open his mouth and tell her how much she meant to him, she started to speak again.

"You lied to me. If not outright, at least by omission. You know how I feel about people—men—not being upfront with me. After the way Maxwell treated me, I vowed no other man would ever lie to me again."

Her words hit him with the force of a sledgehammer and lodged deep in his heart. She backed away from him, a sad, shuttered look on her face. Nicholas knew he was losing her. "Emily, I love you. I want to marry you. Don't do this to us."

"*I* didn't do it, Nicholas. You did. You lied to me. You made a fool of me. I'd never be able to trust you again."

The anger seemed to have drained out of her. Now she just sounded beaten. "But, Emily—"

"I want you to leave my home. Now. Go upstairs, get your things and get out of here. I don't want to see or hear from you again. The case is finished. There's no reason for us to have any more contact."

"For God's sake, Emily, I—"

"Get out, Nicholas."

Nicholas couldn't believe it had gone so wrong. He'd thought she'd cave in when he told her he loved her. He knew she loved him. She wasn't the type of woman to sleep with a man unless her emotions were involved. Yet here she was, ready to give up on them because of a little misunderstanding.

He knew she hated being lied to, but he hadn't realized she was so paranoid about it. Why couldn't she be more reasonable? He'd bared his soul in front of his work colleagues and still she wouldn't listen. Well, he wasn't going to beg. He'd made a big enough idiot of himself as it was.

To hell with it. Who needed love anyway? He'd managed fine before. He would again. There were plenty of women out there. Women who were only after a bit of fun, who didn't want the gold ring and the wedding bells. Women who wouldn't rip his guts to shreds when they rejected his love.

He threw his arms in the air in defeat and slammed across the room. Shouldering Marty and Terry out of the way, he stomped up the staircase to the bedroom. He snapped on the bedside lamp and grabbed his jeans, stepped into them and pulled them up, sliding the zip home so swiftly he was in danger of doing himself an injury.

Ignoring the smear of potting soil on his chest, he dragged a tee shirt over his head. Then he pulled his bag out from under the edge of the bed and stuffed his belongings inside. As he reached into the top drawer of the bedside table to grab his holster, he paused, his gaze on the dish of condoms.

His mind spun back to the night before. Loving Emily, here, in this very bed. God help him, he didn't want to walk away like this, but perhaps it was for the best. If he left her alone for a bit, maybe she'd calm down and he could talk to her later, make her see how much she meant to him.

Yeah, right. His lips twisted into a bitter line. A woman who didn't trust. A crazy professor with an even crazier cat. A woman who couldn't even dress herself properly without looking like a psychedelic Christmas tree. Who needed that?

Grabbing his bag, he headed to the bathroom to collect his shaving gear. He had to get out of here. Before he said something he'd regret.

Car keys in hand, he raced down the stairs and into the living room. Marty and Terry were still there. He picked up both the Glock and the Smith & Wesson and threw them into his bag, zipping it closed. Then he glanced across at Emily.

She had never looked more beautiful. Her hair was in disarray, a dirty smudge of soil on her cheek. Damp earth decorated the front of her nightie and robe. Her feet were bare. She was so damn alluring, he felt his heart shatter, all his dreams smashed like the fragments of broken pottery littering the corner of the room.

Her face caught and held his attention. It was so sad, her eyes filled with tears she refused to allow to fall. Her mouth trembled with some unnamed emotion, although he didn't need to be a rocket scientist to work out what it was.

Betrayal. She thought he'd betrayed her, just like Maxwell had. But he wasn't like that creep. He hadn't meant to hurt her. All he wanted to do was love her and she wouldn't listen to him. Wouldn't forgive him. And right now, he didn't think she ever would.

"Emily?" he whispered.

Emily shook her head, not even looking at him. A single tear escaped to slide down her face. Turning her back on him, she faced the damaged photograph of her parents.

Nicholas gave up. He picked up his bag, dug into the side pocket and retrieved the velvet jeweler's box he'd hidden there. Buying this had been what had kept him so long when he'd gone out and left Marty to baby-sit Emily. He'd almost driven the salesman crazy, making him display each and every ring. He'd been looking for just the right one, a golden topaz that matched her exotic eyes. And finally he'd found it. A square cut yellow topaz surrounded by glittering diamonds. Not that it mattered a damn right now.

He threw the ring box on the couch. "Here, you may as well give this to that weird cat of yours. She can bury it along with the rest of the broken pottery. I was going to ask you to marry me when this case was over, it's no good to me anymore." He regretted the words the moment they were out of his mouth.

Ah, fuck, I sound like a spoilt kid. Shaking his head, he turned and quietly left the room without saying another word, either to Emily or the other agents.

Emily jumped as the front door slammed. Within minutes, she heard the throaty roar of Nicholas's BMW as he gunned the engine.

This was what she wanted, wasn't it? Nicholas gone. Out of her life. Forever. She didn't need a man who lied to her. Why then did it hurt so much?

As the last echo of the roaring engine faded away, Emily turned back to face the room. Marty, with Terry following, came to stand beside her.

"Are you all right, Emily?" Marty had a concerned frown on his face.

She tried a smile, but it came out more as a grimace. "No, I'm not all right, but I will be. I just need time."

"I'm sorry I told you he was gay. We should have been honest with you. At the time, it seemed like a good idea. You were resisting having a man in the house and I thought if you felt threatened by a normal male, you'd accept one who couldn't possibly be interested in you as a woman. So all of this is my fault."

"It doesn't matter whose fault it was, Marty. The damage has been done now."

"But Nick never deliberately lied to you. He—"

"He just didn't tell me the truth," Emily interrupted. "I vowed after Maxwell no man would ever make a fool of me again." She paused, deep in thought. "But I guess I did that all on my own, didn't I? *I* made a fool of me. Nicholas knew right from the start I was attracted to him. If fact, I deliberately set out to change him so I guess I got what I deserved. Poor, stupid Emily."

"Don't so hard on yourself. It's obvious you care about him. Won't you reconsider? Call him and talk to him."

Emily shook her head, unable to speak. How could there be any future for them when she couldn't trust him not to lie to her? She knew she was being unreasonable, but there it was. She'd felt so hurt and betrayed after she'd found out how

Maxwell had used her, she couldn't face something like that happening again.

It had taken her months to regain her confidence in herself after her ex-lover had taken it and trampled it in the dust. She didn't think she had the strength to go through it again.

"I need to be alone now. I appreciate your concern, Marty, but I'd like you and Terry to leave."

"Will you be okay on your own?"

"I'll be fine." She walked them to the front door. They turned to face her as she opened the door wide.

"I'm sorry for my part in this, Emily," Terry said. "If I had kept my big mouth shut, none of this would have happened."

"Don't worry about it. I had to find out either way. Now or later, it doesn't really matter. It doesn't change the fact Nicholas didn't tell me the truth."

Marty took a white business card and pen from his pocket and scribbled something on the card before handing it to her.

"The Agency number is on that and I've written my home number beside it. If you need anything, anything at all, you give me a ring. Even if all you want is a shoulder to cry on, I'm your man. Okay?"

"Okay, Marty." She nodded her head, giving him a wobbly smile. "Thank you for everything."

She stood in the open doorway and watched them leave. The sky was beginning to lighten, the approaching dawn streaking soft fingers of light across the sky.

Amazing how quickly one's life could change. A few hours of darkness and, pow, the future was altered forever. Was it a future she could handle? She wasn't certain, but what choice did she have? She'd sent Nicholas away. Now she had to live with it.

She closed the door, but didn't bother to lock it. There was no need with the burglar apprehended. With a deep sigh, she wandered into the living room. What a mess. The planter stand lay on its side, potting soil and shards of pottery littering the floor around it. Broken glass from her parents' photograph glittered in the overhead light, the patina of the polished floorboards showing through the odd-shaped fragments.

All in all, it looked like a major catastrophe had taken place. But then it had, hadn't it? The death of a dream, no matter how tenuous. No matter how unrealistic.

She'd weathered the emotional storm after Maxwell's departure from her life. She wasn't certain she was strong enough to handle this one. Something told her Nicholas would always hold her heart in the palm of his hand. And every time he squeezed it, the hurting would start all over again.

She pushed the thought away before an encroaching wave of self-pity swamped her. It was no good standing there dwelling on the state of her heart. She needed to do something to keep herself busy. Too busy to think.

There was no point in going back to bed. For one thing, the night was very nearly over and it was almost time to get up again. For another thing, she had a feeling she wouldn't be able to sleep anyway. Her emotions were too raw to allow for peaceful slumber.

She strode over to the windows and pulled back the heavy drapes, letting in the pale light of the new day. She'd clean this mess up. The house could do with a good scrubbing. No time like the present.

Whirling through the kitchen and into the laundry, she shed her filthy robe. She slipped on a pair of sandals she kept there and filled her arms with dustpan and brush, cleaning cloths, bucket and rubbish bags. Trailing the mop after her, she paused at the kitchen sink to fill the bucket with hot water. Then she advanced on the living room like a general going to war.

Within minutes, she'd swept up the debris, placed the planter stand in the hallway to be mended and picked up the cleaning cloth. A wipe over her parents' photograph removed any clinging fragments of glass. She touched the hole left by the bullet. "Sorry, Dad, you'll have to put up with having a second belly button. At least, until I can get you to a photo lab to get the hole fixed."

But who was going to fix the hole in the middle on *her* body? The one that sat right over her heart?

With the mess cleared away and the room dusted, she was ready to wash the polished floors. But first, she needed to fluff the cushions on the couch. As she picked up the first cushion, she saw it. The item she'd heard Nicholas throw moments before he'd left.

She dug it out from where it had fallen between two cushions. It was a velvet jeweler's box. With the little box cradled in her hands, she sank down onto the floor beside the couch and stared at the container in horror, as if it were something that would reach out and attack her. Swallowing the lump that seemed to have lodged in her throat, she slowly opened it.

Nicholas had bought her a ring. An engagement ring. A beautiful topaz surrounded by tiny diamonds. The faceted surface of the stone caught the light and reflected it back to her, making the stone glitter.

With trembling fingers, she lifted it from its velvet bed and slid it on. It fit perfectly, as if made especially for her. Just as carefully, she removed it and placed it back inside its little box, firmly closed the lid and gently curled her fingers around the container. Then she laid her head down on the couch and cried as if her heart were breaking. And right now, she felt as if it were.

She could no longer doubt that Nicholas did in fact love her. After all, no man went out and bought a woman a beautiful engagement ring unless he was serious. But did that really matter? He'd lied to her, just like Maxwell had. Okay, so it was different, but the end result was the same. He'd destroyed her trust. He'd hurt her by not telling her the truth. How could she ever believe in him again?

The tears fell faster, wetting the cushion beneath her head. She couldn't have cared less. Ria jumped up on the couch and curled up beside her head as if to offer comfort. Her pitiful mewling seemed to suggest that she, too, was already missing Nicholas. Emily slid one hand through Ria's soft fur and allowed the misery to totally swamp her.

She cried for a long time. Until the edges of consciousness started to blur and she felt as if she were floating, hovering on the edge of mind-numbing, restorative slumber. She closed her eyes and allowed herself to slide down into the forgiving arms of sleep, where the hurt of the last few hours couldn't reach her and where she could dream of Nicholas and what could never be.

Chapter Fourteen

The sound echoed down through the layers of overpowering darkness cloaking her mind. A steady thumping—like the intense beating of her heart or the heavy pounding of blood through her veins. A voice yelling out. An annoying sound. One that dragged her up from the protective blanket of sleep that cocooned her and kept her from feeling.

The voice continued, reverberating through the corridors of her mind. Growing louder. More persistent. A sound that defied all efforts to resist it. It finally pulled her from the anonymity of sleep and forced her to face the daylight.

"Where are you, Emily? *Emily.*"

Her eyes felt gritty from her pitiful bout of crying. She blinked, once, twice, and a third time before she was able to focus on the person standing in the entrance to the living room. Emily felt as if she'd been drugged and it took all her willpower to throw off the lingering remnants of sleep.

"Miranda? What are you doing here? How did you get in?" Her voice sounded rusty, as if she hadn't used it for a long time.

"What's wrong with you, girl? I've been belting on the front door for the last ten minutes. When there was no reply, I started to get worried. I tried the door and found it unlocked."

She paused for breath before starting again. "What were you thinking of, leaving your front door unlocked? Anything could have happened to you. I mean, what about the person trying to break in here? I thought I'd come in here and find you murdered or something."

Emily used the edge of the couch to help her stand, her cramped limbs screaming at the movement. Sleeping on the floor with your head resting at an impossible angle on a lumpy couch was definitely not the way to go.

She still had the velvet jeweler's box clutched tight in one hand. For some reason, her brain refused to issue the command for her fingers to uncurl and drop it. "As you can see, I'm fine." She tried to stamp life back into her legs.

"Fine? You call this fine?" Miranda moved further into the room, waving a hand at Emily as she stood teetering in front of the couch. "Good gracious, look at you. First I find the door unlocked. Then when I come in here, you're asleep on the floor. I have no idea how long you've been there, but look at the state you're in."

Emily glanced down at herself. She was still wearing the pale pink cotton nightie she'd donned the night before. A dirty brown patch of dried potting mix marred the front of the garment. Soil clung to her fingers, caked around her nails. Her hair hung about her shoulders in untidy clumps and she'd make a bet her crying bout had left her eyes swollen. "Would you believe I'm having a bad hair day?"

Miranda placed a hand on her shoulder. "What's going on? And where's your bodyguard?"

"Gone," was Emily's stark reply.

Her friend pushed her down onto the couch and sat beside her. "I think you'd better tell me what happened."

"I guess you could say we had some excitement here last night."

"Did you catch whoever was trying to break in and steal the papyrus?"

"It was Maxwell. He got himself into trouble with his gambling. Thought he could sell the papyrus and cover the debts."

"Maxwell? *He's* the one who has been doing all this? That rotten, lousy bastard."

"Tell me about it! I thought I'd done with him in my life and he turns around and involves me in something like this. Well, I don't have to worry any longer. I'm pretty sure he'll end up going to jail."

"So where's Nicholas the Sexy?"

"Gone."

"He left you all alone? He should have—"

"I told him to go. I told him I wanted him out of my house and out of my life."

"But why? I thought you had the hots for him."

Emily lifted pain-filled eyes to Miranda. "I love him. More than I ever thought it was possible to love a man. Don't ask me how it happened so quickly, it just did."

"Oh, Emily, I warned you about falling for him. Many a good woman has come to grief trying to 'straighten' a gay man."

"He's not, and never has been, gay."

"I'm sorry? Did you say—"

"He's not gay. One of the other agents told me he was so I'd allow him to stay here in the house with me. Nicholas never bothered to tell me the truth."

"He's not gay." Miranda punched a fist into the air in a gesture of victory. "Hey, that's terrific. Now there's nothing to stand in your way. You can start using up that bowl of condoms upstairs. I thought I'd end up having to throw them out because they're past their use-by date.

"We've already...indulged." Emily turned her head away as she made the admission.

"So why isn't he here with you now? Doesn't he feel the same way you do?"

"He said he loved me." Emily uncurled her fingers and exposed the velvet ring box clutched in her hand. "He bought me this."

Miranda reached over, took the little container from her and snapped open the lid. "Oh, my. This is gorgeous. The topaz is the exact shade of your eyes. I'm so excited for you, girlfriend."

"Don't be. I sent him away."

"Why? I don't understand. You love him. He loves you. He's not gay, so there's nothing standing in the way of your happiness."

"Nothing but a lack of trust."

"Emily, what *are* you talking about?" Miranda shook her head.

"How can I ever trust him? He lied to me. Right from the very beginning. Even after we'd made love, he didn't tell me he wasn't gay. That it had all been a lie to get him in here. It was just a joke. Emily, the crazy professor. Tell her anything and she'll believe it. How could I ever trust him again after that?"

Miranda rose from the couch and paced across the room. She ran her hand through her hair, ruffling the sophisticated curls. "Oh, for the love of God." She moved back to the couch and knelt in front of Emily. “You’re thinking of Maxwell and how he treated you, aren’t you? Emily, I’m a good judge of character and Nicholas is not like that worm, Maxwell.”

“They both lied to me.” Damn it, she didn’t want to talk about this anymore, but Miranda was like a dog with a bone.

“You said Nicholas went along with the whole ‘gay’ thing so you’d take him into your home. Right?” At Emily’s nod, she continued. “Did he say why he didn’t tell you the truth after you two got to know each other?”

“Because of the case. He said he couldn’t tell me until after the case was finished.”

“Well, there you go. The case is now finished, so what’s the problem?”

“But he lied to me.”

“For crying out loud, not all men are the same. I know Maxwell abused your trust. I know he lied to you, but you have to put it behind you. Nicholas is not like that creep. You have to learn to trust again, both in Nicholas and in your love for each other.”

A tear trickled down Emily’s face. “I’m not certain if I can. He made a fool of me,” she whispered.

“You’re telling me it’s not a matter of trust? That it all comes back to pride? Damaged pride? Your pride? You can’t stand the idea he might have been laughing at you. At your gullibility.”

“No, it’s not that...yes, maybe... Oh, I don’t know.” She broke off as more tears followed the first one.

“Trust, Emily. Every relationship has to have trust. Pride makes a very cold bedfellow and a lonely existence.” She grabbed Emily’s hand and yanked her up from the couch. “I want you to go upstairs and have a shower. Then come back down here and I'll have a cup of coffee waiting for you."

Miranda dragged her from the living room and pointed her toward the staircase. "Go. And think about what I've said while you're about it."

Emily trailed slowly up the stairs and into the bedroom. Collecting a change of clothes, she shut herself in the bathroom and flicked on the shower. With the warm water flowing over her tired body, she replayed her conversation with Miranda. Was it simply pride that had sent Nicholas away? She was honest enough to admit maybe that was a part of it. No one liked to be made a fool of, to have people laughing behind their back.

Thoughts of Maxwell and what he had done surfaced. He'd not only destroyed her trust in men, he'd annihilated her confidence in herself as a woman.

She didn't think she was strong enough to put herself on the line like that again. Would she ever be able to forgive Nicholas his lie? And how could she trust anything else he told her was the truth?

Tired of the questions buzzing round and round in her brain, she turned off the shower, dried herself off and slipped into a pair of leggings and tee shirt. She had no idea what color they were. Who cared? There was no one but Miranda to see.

Miranda called to her as she made her way back down the central staircase. "Hey, Emily, you've got a delivery. Where do you want these guys to put it?"

Standing in the doorway at the front of the house were two deliverymen, the name of a local garden center emblazoned across the pockets of their blue shirts. Supported between them was the biggest fern Emily had ever seen. A Boston fern. In a large blue and white glazed pot.

"Come on, lady, where do you want it? It's getting heavier by the minute."

Emily came out of her daze. "Um...ah, bring it in here. I guess it will have to go on the coffee table for the moment."

She guided the men into the living room and directed them to place the plant in the very center of the table. She was oblivious to Miranda signing the delivery docket and the men departing as she sat on the couch in front of the plant and gently lifted the little white card from among the feathery fronds.

Abigail Mark II

The words were written in a bold script intuition told her was Nicholas's handwriting. He'd personally gone along to the garden center as soon as it opened this morning and chosen the new fern. She hugged the card to her chest as tears filled her eyes and overflowed to trickle down her face.

"I'm not certain what the significance of that fern is," Miranda said from the doorway, "but obviously it's important to you. I mean, who cries over a plant? Mind you, I've never met anyone who talks to plants like you do either."

Emily chuckled through her tears. "It's from Nicholas. And he talks to plants too."

Miranda shook her head. "You're both as bad as each other." She came up behind the couch and laid a hand on Emily's shoulder. "Look, I have to go or I'll be late for work. I only came by to see how you were getting on with your project. There's coffee ready in the kitchen. Will you be all right?"

"I have a lot to think about. I guess I need this time on my own to sort a few things out. Yes, I'll be fine. Miranda? Thanks for being there for me."

"Hey, what are friends for?" She gathered up her purse and keys from the end of the couch where she'd thrown them when she'd first come in. "Think about what I said, Emily. Most of us only get one shot at that once-in-a-lifetime love. Don't throw it away because of pride."

Emily continued to sit in front of the new fern, gently brushing at the fronds as she murmured softly to her latest housemate.

Chapter Fifteen

Nicholas slipped his hand into his top pocket and gently touched the delicate piece of jewelry hidden there. He cast a quick glance around the office to make certain no one was watching him before he pulled the earring out. As he held it up by the stud, the little red heart suspended on the silver chain swung back and forth.

Just like his emotions. Back and forth. Anger one moment, abject misery the next. From one extreme to the other. He was so caught up in his thoughts, he wasn't aware of anyone approaching until Marty barked at him.

"Damn it, man, ring the woman." Marty slammed his hand down on the desk in front of Nicholas. "You've been impossible to work with the last two weeks. No one is game to say a word to you for fear they'll get their ears chewed off."

"No."

"What? No, you won't snap at the rest of us any more? Or no, you won't ring Emily?"

"No, I won't ring Emily. It's up to her to make the first move. After all, she was the one who threw *me* out."

"Do you want this woman?"

Nicholas pushed back in his chair as Marty leaned closer, invading his personal space. "Yes," he mumbled, unable to lie to his friend.

"So ring her already. Or go and see her. Because you're driving everyone here up the wall. We can't live with your moods for much longer."

"She doesn't trust me. She thinks I lied to her."

"You did. *We* did. Even if it was for the good of the case, we still lied to her."

"She should make the first move," Nicholas stubbornly reiterated.

"You pair deserve each other." Marty gave a frustrated sigh. "This is nothing but pride talking. And Emily is just as bad."

"How do you know what Emily is thinking? She just—" He broke off at the guilty look that flashed across Marty's face. "You've been in contact with her? Who the fuck gave you the right to interfere in my life?"

Marty backed away, his hands raised to ward off the anger Nicholas knew he was projecting.

"Emily rang *me*, not the other way around."

"What'd she ring you for?" A tiny burst of hope sprang to life deep in his heart.

"She wanted to know how you were doing. I gave her the same speech I just gave you. Now it's up to the pair of you. You want a future with the woman? Do something about it instead of sitting there playing with that earring."

Nicholas watched Marty walk away to collect his jacket. His work colleagues were right. He'd been a grump for the last two weeks. More than that, he'd been a rotten bastard, taking his bad mood out on everyone around him. He hadn't known anything could hurt so much and he'd never dreamed he'd miss anyone as much as he missed Emily. Pain shafted through him whenever he thought of her and that was only every minute of every day.

He lowered his head onto his clenched fist, the same one that held tight to the little red love heart. What a fool he was. He'd handled this all wrong. To hell with pride. He'd go to Emily tomorrow and convince her to give him another chance. He had nothing to lose but his future happiness.

"Get it together, Nick. We've got a farewell dinner to attend. It's not often one of our own gets a transfer to the National Crime Authority."

Nicholas looked up to find Marty standing in front of his desk again. He'd forgotten all about the dinner for Terry. He didn't really feel in the mood for a celebration, but the least he could do was go and have a few drinks with Terry to wish him well.

ꟃ

Emily dialed the number and waited. The moment Miranda picked up the phone, she burst into speech. "I need your help."

"You still wallowing in self-pity? Have you thought about what I said?"

"Please, Miranda. I need your help, not another lecture. You have to come over here right now."

"Is everything all right, Emily?" The tone of Miranda's voice had changed from censure to concern.

"Not yet, but I hope it will be. And that's why you have to come over here and help me. I'll be waiting for you."

Without giving Miranda time to respond, Emily hung up the telephone. Whirling about, she raced up the stairs. First a shower. She could do that while she waited for Miranda.

She showered quickly, shampooing her hair until it was squeaky clean. After drying herself with a thick bath towel, she smoothed jasmine-scented skin lotion all over her body. Next, with the hair dryer turned up on high, she dealt with her wet hair. When it was soft and fluffy about her shoulders, she laid the dryer down on the vanity and stepped back to view herself in the mirror.

"Nicholas, you haven't got a chance," she whispered just as she heard a knock on the front door.

Grabbing the towel and wrapping it around herself, she clattered back down the staircase to let her friend in. "Hurry, Miranda. They'll be at the restaurant by now." Grasping her by the hand, she tugged Miranda up the stairs in her wake.

It wasn't until they'd reached the door of the bedroom that Miranda recovered her wits enough to plant her feet and refuse to go any further without answers.

"Whoa. What the heck's going on here?"

"I'm going to Nicholas and I need your help."

"Well, about time, girl. What changed your mind? Last I heard, you wouldn't even think about giving the guy a second chance. What's different now?"

"Me!" Emily shrugged. "You were right. It was nothing but pride. I couldn't stand the idea he was laughing at me behind my back, just like Maxwell did."

She held up her hand as Miranda opened her mouth to speak. "Don't get me wrong. I'm still scared I might get hurt again, but you know what? It'll be worth it if it means there's a chance I can have Nicholas in my life. It just took me two weeks to get past my hurt pride." She grinned. "I never said I was the brightest light bulb in the pack."

Miranda chuckled. "You academics are all alike. Real life defeats you every time. I'm glad to see you finally came to your senses. But what do you need my help for?"

"I need you to turn me into a raving beauty."

Miranda chuckled. "Emily, you *are* a raving beauty. You just don't take the time to emphasize your good points."

"And that's why I need you. For once, I don't want to look like an artist's palette gone wrong. I want to look sophisticated and sexy. The type of woman Nicholas would go for." She spun away and retrieved underwear from the chest of drawers. "While I put these on, you go through my wardrobe and find me something sexy to wear."

She shut herself in the bathroom and slipped into the black suspender bikini panties and matching bra she'd bought when Nicholas had taken her shopping. Then she joined Miranda in the bedroom, grinning at her friend's wolf whistle.

"Too much, you think?" Propping her fisted hands on her hips, she posed in the doorway.

"Never." Miranda burst out laughing. "The man is not going to know what hit him." She held up the dress she'd selected. "This will go perfectly with the black underwear."

"I can't wear that. It's too—"

"Sexy?" Miranda raised her eyebrows. "Isn't that what you want?"

Emily stared at the dress. It was one she'd bought on an impulse and never worn, figuring it was too much for her staid professor image. It was made of a slinky fabric, black shot through with silver thread. Sleeveless, rounded neck, it looked like nothing spectacular until it was on. Then it hugged the body like a second skin, ending a good few inches above the knee.

Miranda was right. It *was* a sexy dress. Just what the occasion called for. A mischievous grin curved her lips. "Oh yeah, bring it on, maestro."

She sat while Miranda swirled her hair up into a confection of curls atop her head, fastening it in place with a diamante clasp. It was all she could do to contain her impatience while Miranda made up her face, emphasizing the exotic tilt of her eyes and enhancing the mysterious topaz color.

With that finished, she sat on the side of the bed and carefully eased on black, lace-top stockings, fastening the suspenders firmly. Shiny black high-heel shoes completed the preparations. With a deep breath, she stepped into the dress and turned so Miranda could zip her up.

"Wow." She stared at herself in the full-length mirror. "Is that really me?"

"Girl, you're going to knock him dead." Miranda gathered up her car keys and gave Emily a quick hug. "Hey, I'm out of here. I've got my own man to see to tonight." As she disappeared out the bedroom door, she called back, "And don't forget, I expect an invitation to the wedding."

Conscious of time passing, Emily grabbed a small black evening bag from the wardrobe and tucked her keys, wallet and a handkerchief inside. She was ready, although she couldn't resist a final glance in the mirror.

All of a sudden, she paused, hit by a startling revelation. The reflection in the mirror was of a sexy, alluring woman. A sophisticated woman of the world. But it wasn't her. It wasn't Emily.

Quickly, before she lost the courage, she unclipped the suspenders and slid one stocking off before rifling through the drawer for another to take its place. The one she pulled out looked green to her, but she knew it wasn't. She didn't own any green stockings. One thing she *was* certain of, it wasn't black.

Hands shaking, she rolled the stocking up her leg and fastened it in place. Then she grabbed her evening bag and the velvet jeweler's box and tottered on her high-heels down the stairs to call a taxi. Locking the front door firmly behind her, she hovered impatiently until the taxi arrived.

The drive to the restaurant was fraught with tension. Emily's palms grew damp with nervousness. When they arrived at the restaurant in downtown Sydney, she had difficulty extracting the right amount of money to pay the driver. Taking a deep breath to still her racing heart, she entered the restaurant in search of Nicholas.

She spotted him immediately, sitting between Terry and Marty at a center table. Several other men had joined them, all enjoying the farewell dinner for Terry. She thanked God for Marty and his interference. If he hadn't left his business card on that fateful night, she would never have known how to get in contact with him. Federal agents didn't exactly have easily accessible phone numbers.

And if she hadn't spoken to him today, she wouldn't have known exactly where to find Nicholas tonight. Two weeks ago, Nicholas had laid his heart on the line in front of his work colleagues and she'd rejected it. It was only fair she make her declaration in just as public a way.

A loud wolf whistle from one of the men made her smile, but it was the look on Nicholas's face that captured her attention.

He'd been about to take a sip of his drink when he'd spotted her. His mouth dropped open in shock, the drink suspended before his face, the glass tilted. As she reached the table, he recovered himself enough to lower the glass back to the table.

"Hello, Nicholas." Her voice was husky, desire clawing at her insides at the sight of him.

When he would have stood, she pressed her hand down on his shoulder to keep him in his seat. She opened her evening bag and pulled out the ring box, snapping it open and extending it toward him, a smile on her face. "Nicholas Farley, I love you and I trust you with my life. Will you marry me?"

Nicholas tried to swallow, but his throat had gone dry. His hand trembled as he reflexively took the velvet box from Emily. He couldn't believe she was here. Particularly when he'd only just made the decision to go and see her tomorrow.

"Emily, what are you doing here?"

"I came to see *you*. Marty told me you'd be here tonight."

He tried again to rise to his feet, only to have Emily once again push him back into his chair. "Um, shouldn't we go somewhere private to have this conversation?"

She shook her head. "No, if you can do it in public, so can I. This way, you'll know I mean business."

Then she shocked him by going down on one knee in front of him. His mouth quirked as he suddenly realized what she was doing. She had reversed the order of things. Where tradition said the man must go on bended knee to ask his love to marry him, now Emily was doing it. In light of the fact he'd already told her he wanted to marry her, it was a novel approach. One destined to get his attention.

"I'm sorry for what I did to you," she whispered. "I know you didn't deliberately lie to me, that it was all because of the case. But mostly, I'm sorry I didn't trust you."

She paused, a hand pressed to her heart as if in pain. "I love you, Nicholas. I promise to trust you and keep faith with you all the days of my life. Will you put me out of my misery and marry me?"

Emily watched as Nicholas pulled the ring out of the box. He reached out and took the hand resting over her heart, sliding the ring home. She marveled again at the perfect fit. A bit like her and Nicholas. The perfect match.

A gasp escaped as lifted her up to sit on his lap, his arms tight about her waist. Emily felt like she'd finally come home.

"I can't think of anything I'd like better than to marry you and spend the rest of my life with you." He turned her face up to his and captured her lips in a soul-shattering kiss.

Suddenly it was as if her blood had caught fire. Her mouth surrendered to his and she trembled at the erotic stroke of his tongue as he drove home the message that he truly did love her.

The need for oxygen finally drove them apart and Emily surfaced to find Marty and the other men around the table clapping and whistling wildly. She glanced up at Nicholas to catch his wide grin and raised eyebrows. "What?"

"Do you know you've got two different colored stockings on?"

"I know. It was deliberate. If you take me, you take me as I am. Color blindness, quirky behavior, crazy cat and all."

"Sweetheart, I wouldn't have you any other way." He shrugged. "I kind of like the bright pink stocking. It makes a statement." He dropped a quick kiss on her lips before going on. "There is one thing, Emily. Married life with you and Ria will never be boring."

Then he claimed her lips again in a kiss she felt all the way down to her toes. The last thing she was conscious of before she gave herself up to the feel of his mouth was the catcalls from the men around the table and Marty's whispered words. "Way to go, Emily. That's sure one way to initiate Nicholas into the joys of loving a woman."

Oh yeah! Project: Man had been an unqualified success.

About the Author

To learn more about Alexis Fleming please visit www.alexisfleming.net Send an email to Alexis at alexisfleming@hotmail.com or join her Yahoo! group to join in the fun with other readers as well as Alexis! http://groups.yahoo.com/group/AlexisFlemingandFriends

Look for these titles

Now Available

Stud Finders Inc.
A Handyman's Best Tool
Emerald Ice

Coming Soon:

Mortified Matchmakers

Together they find a special love—
can it survive the threat stalking her?

Giving Chase

© 2006 Lauren Dane

Some small towns grow really good looking men! This is the case with the four Chase brothers. The home grown hotties are on the wishlist of every single woman in town and Maggie Wright is no exception.

Maggie has finally had it with the men she's been dating but a spilled plate of chili cheese fries drops Shane Chase right into her lap. The sheriff is hot stuff but was burned by a former fiancée and is quite happy to play the field.

After Shane's skittishness sends him out the door, Maggie realizes that Kyle Chase has had his eye on her from the start. Now that Shane has messed up, Kyle has no intention of letting anything stop him from wooing her right into his bed.

Despite Maggie's happiness and growing love with Kyle, a dark shadow threatens everything—she's got a stalker and he's not happy at all. In the end, Maggie will need her wits, strength and the love of her man to get her out alive.

Shana thought going on a job interview was going to be tough, she had no idea it could cost her life.

Spitfire

© 2006 Arianna Hart

Getting the chance to rescue computer guru Royce Renault's kidnapped niece is the opportunity of a lifetime for Private Investigator wanna be Shana Quinn. But when the kidnappers come after her will this be the last opportunity she ever gets?

Available now in ebook and print from Samhain Publishing.